Beyond the Teacups

 Formatted with Vellum

Beyond the Teacups

HAILEY RENEE

For those who've wrestled with the weight of anxiety, who've felt lost in the shadows of their own thoughts.

May you one day know what it feels like to be truly seen, truly understood, and deeply loved in return.
This is for <u>you</u>.

Playlist

Run - Joji (*Dedicated to past "me"*)
The Lumineers - Salt And The Sea
Hozier - Hymn to Virgil
Jeff Buckley - Lover, You Should've Come Over
Chris Stapleton - Starting Over (*Dedicated to current "me"*)

Disclaimer

This story is not your typical lighthearted escape, and its pacing reflects the nature of it being a shorter book. While there is romance and a fast-moving plot, this is a deeply layered narrative that delves into real, raw mental health struggles, particularly anxiety, and the profound impact it can have on a person's life.

The main character's journey goes beyond romantic entanglements. She is grappling with the loss of a parent, the weight of parental expectations, and internal battles that many of us endure but don't often discuss openly. This portrayal is an honest look at how anxiety can shape someone's world. Moments of hope are present but are hard-earned and far from effortless.

The story addresses challenging themes, including exposure therapy and the overwhelming intensity of anxiety. There is a pivotal moment where the character "snaps," but it's important to note that this is not a neat or definitive resolution. Healing is rarely linear; it's messy, long, and unpredictable.

At its heart, this is a story about embracing the reality that it's okay not to have everything figured out. It's okay to ask for help. It's okay to take small steps toward healing. Most importantly, it's okay to keep going, even when it feels impossible.

If you're looking for a romance entwined with the struggles of real life, this book offers something powerful, raw, and deeply meaningful. Please read with care and an open heart.

Love always,

Hailey Renee

A Sip Before

The rich aroma of pumpkin and chocolate wafts through the air, wrapping me in a familiar embrace. My hands move without thinking, instinct guiding me as I scoop the thick pumpkin mixture into perfect cookies, their soft, warm texture beneath my fingertips. It's a routine as old as the walls of this house—mix, bake, display, repeat.

Add the constant rhythm of tea brewing, kettles filling, and clinking teacups. The kitchen is eerily quiet today, except for the gentle crinkling of parchment as I slide freshly baked cookies onto it. I take in this moment's warmth and sweet comfort, letting it settle around me. Yet, as I begin to put the cooled cookies into small brown paper bags, I can't shake the weight of something pressing down on me . . .

A restlessness, a question, something that returns repeatedly, like a whisper carried on the wind. I glance around at the renovated first floor of my childhood home, now a beautiful tea and bakery shop. The mismatched teacups, the old wooden beams, the shelves filled with jars of tea, spices, and little trinkets—it's all mine. Every corner of this place is shaped by my hands, my heart. But . . . is this it?

Is this all there will ever be?

"What if everything changes?" The words slip from my lips, barely more than a breath. I pause, staring down at the row of neatly packed cookies. My voice sounds strange and foreign, as if it belongs to someone else. "What if there really is more than this?"

The thought lingers in the air, both unsettling and exhilarating.

I did not welcome the change.

Chapter One

OPHELIA

Music floods from the record player in the corner of the room, wrapping me in its melody. Something about a good tune really sets the mood.

My wooden worktable has a patchwork of small bowls scattered about, filled with dried herbs and fragrant tea leaves. The comforting smell of chamomile mingles with the sharper, citrusy zest of the dried orange peels—a combination I have been toying with for a few weeks.

Today, I'm determined to get it just right. I add a pinch of lemon balm for a mild, soothing undertone and just the faintest sprinkle of dried hibiscus to blend the color once steeped. I am excited. This looks stunning already. As I work, the rhythm of my movements has my skirt twirling around my legs. I try to ignore the tiny swats from my one-eyed cat, dashing back and forth. Nothing was going to stop me from perfecting this blend today.

The kettle whistles, pulling me from my thoughts. I reach for a teacup off the wooden shelf and filled it with hot water. The dried ingredients began to unfurl and tint the liquid a soft peach. The scent wafting up was delicate but intriguing—a hint of citrus blanched by the mellow sweetness of chamomile.

I hold the cup, inhaling the deepest breath before taking the first sip. Warmth spreads through me as the flavors dance on my tongue. It wasn't perfect, not yet, but it was close. I grab my journal and jot down a quick note:

Chamomile and orange peel base.
Needs a touch more . . . brightness? Maybe some mint?

I paused, tapping the pen against my lips. The music still envelops my soul in peace as I clean up a few of the messy areas of my work table before preparing myself for yet another round of trial and error with this blend.

It is so close to being perfect. I reach for another scoop of chamomile when my music abruptly stops. I'm stunned back into reality, suddenly aware of the thundering crashes in my chest as my heart rate quickens.

I look at my wristwatch. It's still two hours before the teahouse opens to the townsfolk, but I did leave the front door unlocked in case any of the homeschool co-ops wanted to spend their early morning sessions enjoying some free baked goods reheated from last night's run.

I turn into the main room, but nothing prepares me for the impending doom in the corner—Emmett Sterling.

"Did someone order mail?" Emmett says in an icy voice.

I look at his hands, praying to anyone who would listen that a package would accompany the letters, but no. He holds a singular pink envelope.

"Are all mailmen this invasive?" I ask, shooting him a look, though the racing in my chest is not letting up, and my fingers feel tingly.

"Only the good-looking ones." He winks.

I coach myself through the want-to-gag, but he catches my hunch.

"Ophelia Mossgrove, are you repulsed?" He huffs as he tosses the envelope on a nearby table.

I hesitate but ultimately go through the sea of chairs to get it. *Wool & Whisker's Vet Services* was in bold on the front. I process this before doing something I wouldn't normally consider—I send the envelope flying into the man before me, and it hits his chest with a pathetic thump before delicately falling to the ground.

My eyes widen as I realize I just assaulted the mailman. Well, Emmett Sterling who happens to be the mailman, but still.

"Did you just throw mail at me?" He bends to grab the letter on the floor.

I don't answer. I have an anxiety attack on speed dial and a tea blend that needs perfecting. Emmett would not get the best of me today, but the replies were loading in my head on autopilot.

He smiles. "Oh, I see, reverting to the cottage in your head to avoid the charming man in front of you?"

My cheeks flush pink before I twirl around, a last-ditch effort to stick it to him. With all the emotion I can muster, I whip my head back and spit out, "You can't even deliver mail correctly. Nothing about you is charming,"

With that, I disappear back into the kitchen. My heart feels like it's making its way up my throat, my eyes pulse, and my fingers tingle. Something about that man makes me feel so angry, but maybe it was because I have been dealing with him and his inability to deliver mail correctly for the past five months. I need the package he claims was lost, but I know he misdelivered it, and someone is bound to return it to the post office.

At least, that is what I keep hoping for. I look at my watch again—an hour and a half before opening.

Perfect. I could spend another half hour on the blend and then an hour prepping for opening. I am so thankful I woke up as early as I did. Getting ready before the sun came out was never fun, but having my mornings to myself really fulfills my soul. It wouldn't be too long before the rare lull of this silence was replaced with the bustling sounds of townsfolk and their all-too-familiar orders.

I peek around the corner once more. The spot where Emmett once stood is now empty. I hear the rumble of his truck exiting the gravel driveway. *Thank God.* I twirl around and replace the silence with music as I dance my way back to the kitchen, humming and returning to the rhythmic adventure that was tea making.

Okay, let's do this . . . *again.* I reach for another scoop of chamomile, the same amount of orange peels, a dash of lemon balm, and a whisper of mint. My fingers trace the bowl's rim as if sealing the moment into memory. *Let's see if you are as perfect as you look.*

I add more water to the kettle and adjust the knob as I inspect the flame to put it just right. I lean against the counter. Poe is sunbathing in the filtered light cascading from the back door window.

I have so much to do as the fall season rolls in. Decorating, curating a new menu, decluttering the storage room, and my least favorite task . . . an oil change for my sweet Chevy, which is bunkered out there in the impending cold. The hum of the kettle blankets my nerves like an encouraging friend. I fill the teacup once again with hot water. The steam curls upward, the scent blooming thicker than last time. The water expanded with a golden hue kissed with pink.

The cup's warmth spreads through my palms, and I let my lips land on the rim, slowly sipping the liquid. Bright, gentle, inviting—the aroma is divine. I set the cup down, vibrating with excitement. I scoop Poe up and hold him high in the air. *"We did it! That's it!"*

I did it, but he was the emotional support I needed. I look

around, eyeing my notebook before jotting down several almost unreadable words: *Name: Haven's Bloom.*

I toss the pen on the counter. Now, we need to make a few dozen muffins . . .

5

Chapter Two

EMMETT

My truck hums as I idle in the post office parking lot. My muscles tense at the thought of another heavy load tomorrow. This season has a way of suffocating a man in the mail business.

I finally found the courage to exit my truck, plunging into whatever chaos was in the office that evening. The bell above the door chimes, and I glance around at the eyes now watching me. There are a few faint smiles, but one looming character sits in the back, waiting for the right moment to strike. Her eyes peer into my soul—my sister.

Her purple hair stands out amongst the sea of browns and blondes. She is grinning wickedly at me as she holds up a box that looks to be the size of a small child.

"Emmy, I think you forgot something." She sets the box down. "At the wrong address, like always."

Not this again. I reach for the box, tossing it up in the air, then spinning it to see the address.

"Wow, be careful, weirdo, that says *fragile*." She playfully kicks me.

I pretend to drop the box, catching it at the last minute.

"Oh, hush. This is kind of what I do for a living," I snort, though inside, a part of me aches. I've spent the last two years running a successful farm-to-table business called *Aspen Farms*.

I mentioned it was successful, right? Because it was—until it wasn't.

Let's just say you can never run a business built on a crumbly foundation—and that was what Aspen Farms was—crumbly.

Rebuilding that land after the flood would take just about all I had and then some. The only option for the foreseeable future was Havenwood—*home sweet home*, as some would call it.

Me? I am still healing, I guess. Morgan must have seen the look on my face because hers softens as she steps back.

"How are you doing?" she asks. It comes out awkward, but I can feel the genuineness from her.

"Eh, you know what they say." I throw my hands up. "You can tune a piano but can't tuna fish."

I slap my thigh and make my best impression of our dad's laugh. I can tell I nailed it because her face scrunches up in embarrassment. I peer down at the box, finally figuring out who I must apologize to. *Ophelia Dawn Mossgrove* is printed in a funny font across the top.

Imported from Poland. Oh, you have to be kidding me. This day just got a million times better. Do I get to visit the feisty herbalist *again*? Take my money! I ignore Morgan's words, grabbing my lunch bag from the employee fridge and the package and dashing out the back and around the building to my truck.

This is going to be interesting.

My truck struggles on the final turn as I pull sharply onto the familiar gravel driveway. Ophelia pretends to hate me, but deep down, she fancies my company.

A company that isn't often shared, but when it is, I hate to admit it, I like it. Her banter keeps my mind busy, and I enjoy toying with her. Something about making her angry makes me laugh—but all in good fun.

Though, the mail mishaps . . . that is something I haven't addressed with her.

How do you tell a woman she is too distracting? Especially someone as eclectic and firm as Ophelia? I put my truck in park and turn down the radio. A quick glance at the time would indicate she'd just closed up. But if I know her well enough, and much like the rest of the townsfolk, she is likely still inside offering baked goods or helping someone with something like she always does.

Movement under her truck catches my eyes, and I see a pair of light green cowboy boots thrashing back and forth. I sprint into action, throwing my knees to the ground, wincing at the pain of the gravel biting my skin. I steady myself enough to pull whoever it was out from beneath.

Soft whimpers escape, then a terribly loud belly laugh.

"Ophelia?" I look down at the woman below me, her neck drenched in oil, which is splattered on her cheek and smeared across her eyebrow. Her eyes meet mine, and her mouth, once a smile, now a thin line.

My heart races and I can only muster a breathy, "What the hell are you doing, Mossgrove?" Not a single sound comes back in return. "I see you are still not talking to me."

She uses the truck to steady herself as she stands and catches a glimpse of herself in the window. "I–I was doing an oil change."

I chuckle, "More like the oil change was doing you."

I reach under the truck and grab the oil pan, kicking it into place—not that it would be helpful at this point. "Go on, get inside. I will finish this."

It wasn't a question—whether she'd have it or not—it was getting done, and *not* by the little lady in front of me wearing the weirdest color boots known to man.

She hesitates before her shoulders slump, and she twirls to walk away.

This shouldn't take too long. I can pop the package on her

patio and go home. My stomach rumbles at the thought of the steak and fries from *The Barkeeps* waiting for me in the fridge. I notice how rusted her jack stands are, chuckling to myself again. *What an Ophelia thing to do.* I apply a thin coat of oil to the new filter seal, install it, and replace the drain plug.

I looked around for the funnel I saw rolling in the gravel from the heavy wind. Retrieving it from its adventure, I use the funnel to add oil, replacing the oil cap before the painstaking removal of the rusted jack stands and getting her truck lowered and off the floor jack.

Soft hums leak from the upstairs windows, accompanied by flashes of shadows. I wipe my hands off on my jacket as best I can before grabbing the package from my truck.

By this time, Ophelia peeks out of the front door, likely curious if I took off or kept my word.

"Well, look at you, practically a whole new woman," I say.

All I could see is her wet hair dangling as she sticks her head out. Her eyes light up as I wiggle the package for attention. I liked that look. As I near the patio, she opens the door, ready to take her package.

For a moment, I step back. She was . . . different—not the woman I'd come to see most days—the one with a smudge of flour on her cheek, some herbal oil in her hair, always in an over-sized sweater and an apron. Her hair was loose, framing her soft face.

Her cheeks flush, and her usual layered dress replaced with a fitted one. It clings to her curves in a way I don't usually register. I caught myself staring, so I fix my gaze on the box and set it on the patio, sliding it a little toward her. "Your package finally arrived."

She glares at me, weary. "Or you finally decided to stop hoarding it for my torture and returned it to the rightful owner."

No words escape my lips.

She grins for a moment before trying to carry the package in. I enjoy watching her struggle momentarily before saving her big toe from the fifteen-pound package threatening to smash it.

"No response to that, huh?" She shoots another grin while I set the package on the first table I see.

"It may come as a surprise, Mossgrove, but not every day do I feel the need to be a smartass, but especially not when my stomach is eating itself." I slap my hand on my grumbling abdomen, feeling a tad lightheaded. My pocket vibrates. I check my phone, and a string of messages appear, all related to reminders my dad set up for the family chat. I roll my eyes as I slip my phone back into my pocket, now greeted by Ophelia, arms stretched, holding out a sandwich.

"Eat," she says, setting the sandwich on the table beside me. "It's pot roast. If you want cheese, let me know. I can add some."

She sways back and forth to the soft music playing in the corner. She's a unique person—always has been.

Sorry, steak and fries, tomorrow, I'll eat you. I grab the pot roast sandwich, and I'm immediately put into a trance by the thick smell of roast and buttered bread. What a beautiful sandwich. I try to act unfazed as I bite into something crafted from the heavens. The roast melts in my mouth as it blends with the soft bun. This is, in fact, the best sandwich I've ever eaten.

Be cool, Emmett. "Thanks." I look at her.

She's studying me, trying to see where my mask will slip. I hear Florence, a family friend of hers, walking in from the back door. *Sorry, little lady, not today.* "Well, it's only fair. I did finish your hack job of an oil change," I say, and with that, I did what she did to me this morning. I twirl around and leave —but of course, with that delicious sandwich.

Chapter Three

OPHELIA

Emmett leaves, the screen door falling shut behind him.

I let myself linger on it for a moment before turning to the eyes staring holes into my head.

Florence sits in the corner of the room on an old wing-back chair—velvet green. Her wild orange curls stand out against the coloring of the velvet. She sips her coffee—which she always brings herself—and eats a cream cheese pumpkin muffin for which she left cash under the tray.

I smile. Her bubbly personality oozes, and the smell of her incense-infused perfume is familiar and comforting. I love her. It's way past closing, but Flo was welcome anytime, so long as she didn't comment about my appearance not being that of my morning hour energy, though judging by her pajamas and the look on her face, I don't think she cares one bit.

Today is a special day, though the meaning still aches in my mind. She sips her coffee. When her eyes drift to the window, I use it as an excuse to dip back into the kitchen. I dig around the fridge for the carrot cake I baked in preparation for today.

I grab some twine from the junk drawer and tie a rustic bow. As I approach, Florence looks like she is in another world, her mind likely running a million miles per hour. I softly reach for her hand. She jumps at the contact.

"Hi, Flo," I say, voice low. "I baked you something sweet enough to take those blues away."

She takes the plate, putting on the best smile she can manage. It takes her a moment to register what it is, but the moment she does, the misty eyes make an appearance.

"Alan's favorite . . ." She presses her lips together, looking out the window and back to me. "That old man is missing his own birthday." She whispers, her best attempt at lightening the mood.

I let out a giggle. "What an Alan thing to do."

I let her hand go, giving her another smile as I pull a candle from my pocket. "Here."

Her eyes threaten to boil over with tears.

"You don't have to do it here, but honor his life in good memories," I say as I let the candle fall into her open palm.

Alan had been a brilliant man. Between him and my father, I'd been set. He taught me how to fix simple things around the house and would help me with anything as long as he got his carrot cake as payment. When we lost him, it felt like losing another dad all over again.

Memories fog my brain, and I feel myself slipping into that darkness.

I feel a hand on mine. "I love you, Angel." Florence kisses my forehead.

Florence and my mom have been friends since high school. It was always funny growing up to see my mom hang out with someone so opposite to her. Mom was an orchard worker, taking over her dad's business most of her life. Once her parents passed away, she retired and now manages a small cut flower garden business out of the town next to us, Rosewood. I see her every Sunday, and we often talk on the phone, but I will admit it is nice to have Flo around when I need motherly love.

I watch her as she tucks the candle between the tied twine. "I will savor this later. I may even visit the ole man," she says, eyes shiny.

I give her a half smile. Flo may have wanted to visit Alan, but deep down inside, I knew she wouldn't go. She always says it never felt like he was there, that she was sitting on the cold ground talking to nothing. She would talk about feeling him most in her shop, knowing he was somewhere tinkering with a broken antique in the afterlife, and I could understand this.

I knew my dad was somewhere riding his motorcycle down a country road, blaring his tunes. I put my hand on her shoulder, catching her eyes as she looked up.

"You do what you feel brings you happiness, Flo," I say. "He wouldn't want you visiting that grave. He would have wanted you to play a good card game with the girls and drink whatever you guys have in those mugs. That was where he would find you, with that smile that melted him. Do that tonight." I pat her hand and watch as she turns her frown into a smile.

She hugs me. "Speaking of which! Come play some cards with me and the girls sometime. I know we are old, but we sure know how to play a mean game of cards!"

I smiled at the thought.

As she gets up, she looks outside and takes in the view. "Fall sure is coming fast, if not already here. I don't know. I never understood the whole 'official fall' thing." She shakes her head.

"October is more promising," I say.

Florence looks at me, "That is next week, sugar!"

What? I haven't even begun my to-do list.

Well, aside from the oil change, we aren't going to talk about that.

"Hmm, seems as though my Saturday will be spent decorating the outside of my home for the upcoming holiday. I'm behind . . ." I drift off into thought, not finishing my sentence.

"The Fall Festival is going to be the biggest yet," Flo begins. "We have Gage from the bar hosting the live music, and I hear it will feature some local music artists. We even have a budget this year to add more vendors. You wouldn't be one of those vendors, would you?" She treads lightly, peeking up at me through her vibrant orange curls.

"Likely not, Flo, but you already knew that," I say, keeping my eyes on her.

"Oh, come on, Sugar, there is so much more out there waiting for you with this festival! More exposure, maybe even some nearby townspeople looking for business partners. You know, maybe even a good gentleman out there looking for muffins . . . and a wife?"

I twirl around on my feet, and as I walk away, I turn my head back to see her standing in the doorway to leave as I say, "Everything I need is right here."

Florence ponders my words and accepts them for now. "Well, thanks again for the carrot cake. I love you bunches. See you in the morning, Sugar." She lets the screen door open as she leans against it, smiling.

"I love you more, Flo." My heart warms. She shuts the main front door with it. She already knows it's time for me to retire to my chambers, as she calls it. On Fridays, I close early. It used to be because I would help my dad with his parts shop on Friday afternoons, but now it just stuck, even after he was gone.

The music leaking from the record player hits my ears. Taking a deep breath, I weave in and out of the tables and chairs in the front room. I can't shake the rhythm, so I let out small sways, feeling the lyrics. My feet take over as I dance lightly in the open spaces.

My hum becomes soft singing, and my soft singing becomes a powerful belt. I can feel my singing vibrating in my chest. All the anxiety of the day seeps from my soul, disappearing with each twirl. I gather all the dishes and place them in the sink for washing. I gracefully navigate all the baked goods, putting them in airtight containers and marking them with the day and time.

Someone from the local homeschool co-op will pick them up tomorrow morning, as she usually does. The homeschoolers love my baked treats.

After finishing the remainder of the closing chores, I look around the kitchen to admire the cleanliness, as I did in the main room.

Catching a glimpse of myself in the china hutch glass, I freeze.

I look like death.

My hair is a sweaty mess. There's flour on my black dress, and my cheeks are red from the day's stress.

I just showered. A bath would do.

A bath, a book, and some hot chocolate. The standard is wine and a book, but nothing about me is standard. I ready my hot chocolate and make my way to the stairs. Looking up at the steps before me, I take a deep breath and begin the journey. As I step into my bedroom, I am instantly enveloped by the warmth and elegance of the space.

The walls are painted a deep, soothing green, which brings out the richness of the wooden furniture I have scattered about. With its ornate, carved headboard, the bed feels inviting and stately, draped in soft white linens and accented with plush, green velvet pillows. I glance at the foot of my bed. The tufted bench sits, perfectly matching the restful, muted tones of the room.

Goodness, my bed looks inviting, but no – I must take a bath.

As I secure my claw clip, I pull my hair up, twisting it into a loose bunch. The clip tugs at a few too-tight hairs, and I wince. I let out a slow, steady breath as I pad barefoot across the bathroom floor, eager for the day's tension to be rid entirely from my body. I turn the faucet and watch as the bath water fills the tub. Reaching for the rose petals on the tub's edge, I scatter a few in the water.

As I slip out of my dress and into the bath, the warmth of the water immediately wraps around me, loosening the tension in my muscles. I sink deeper, letting the water rise to my neck then my cheeks. My mind drifts to the mailman, his lingering gaze, his cheek covered in the juices from the pot roast sandwich, and the soft and delicate way he grabbed the sandwich from the table.

I push the thoughts away, trying to relax, but the memory of his eyes watching me won't leave. Could it be possible for there to be more to this connection? Or am I just reading too much into a rare, nice moment with Emmett, who should mean nothing to me?

I open my eyes, hoping the walls will whisper an answer.
Silence.

Chapter Four

EMMETT

I smell coffee.

Which is odd because I am in bed and at home . . . *alone.*

I turn to look at the clock. Hmm . . . early morning. Gunner, my loyal beagle, didn't bark, which means one thing —Dad.

I toss the sheet off my body, the cold air attacking my bare chest. I reach for my flannel thrown over the end of my bed and head for the bathroom. I look in the mirror. My long dark hair curls at the roots and softens as it gets closer to the ends. I usually keep it in a "man bun," as my sister calls it, but it's been down lately. The fall chill won't be attacking my ears this year. Not when this thick fortress of hair is there to protect them.

I brush a few strands from my face and brush my teeth. The day was going to be interesting if my dad was here uninvited.

"Emmy boy! Awake, are we? Day off today, huh?" He stands from the chair at my kitchen island.

I roll my eyes, seeing he has helped himself to a bagel

from Ophelia's that my sister brought me. A fire in me begins, but it evaporates when I see his face. He looks . . . unwell.

"Hard to sleep when an intruder makes you coffee." I point at the mugs sitting on the island beside him.

"Your cup is still warm," he says as he presses his fingers to the outside of the glazed mug. "I don't like using my spare key, but this . . . well, I need to talk to you." He sips his coffee, avoiding eye contact.

I sit with his words. What in the hell could this be about? Was this when he finally laid into me about being a failure? My stomach turns. I try to form words, but nothing comes out. Even at this moment, I feel like a small version of myself. So, I sip my coffee, letting the silence become deafening. However, my mind doesn't swallow itself into a black hole like it's done so well for years as I avoided these one-on-ones with him.

Instead, I am sitting here, playing with childhood memories. I see my dad and Ophelia's dad in the garage, hunched over their motorcycles, their hands smeared with grease, sharing easy laughter. The faint scent of motor oil and summer heat fills the air as if I were standing there now. I remember sitting cross-legged in the driveway, tinkering with my toy car, watching them with wide eyes.

They seemed larger than life back then, as if they could fix anything and everything.

And then there was Ophelia, just a girl in a field of wildflowers, her hair catching the light of the late afternoon sun as she twirled, arms wide open, letting the world wrap around her.

I don't think she even noticed me then. But I saw her. I always notice her.

My dad worked the same way he lived—relentlessly. He managed the town like a captain steering a ship through a storm, never resting and constantly pushing forward. I used to sit on the town hall steps, watching him through the window as he leaned over his desk, his brow furrowed in concentration. I thought he was indestructible, but now I see it differently.

He wasn't indestructible. He was wearing himself down, brick by brick, until nothing was left. The memories feel warm and sharp, like they're trying to tell me something I'm not sure I want to hear.

I remember my dad teaching me how to be "like him." I didn't understand until much later. There was no grand speech, no defining moment. It was in the everyday things—waking me up before dawn to help with the dairy chores, showing me how to balance a bucket of feed without spilling it all over myself.

"Strong hands don't mean much if you don't have a strong mind to match," he'd say, his voice steady, calm. He taught me how to change the oil in the truck, crouched next to me in the garage, his hands moving with practiced precision.

"Pay attention," he'd say when my gaze wandered, his tone a mix of patience and authority.

My gaze always wandered to her. *Ophelia.* Always around but never the center. She was like the breeze—something you felt, not something you could catch. She'd be off in her little world while our families had dinner together. My dad and Willie would be hootin' and hollerin' about something or another, but my mind would be full of . . . her.

I can still see her sitting on the living room floor, her feet in the air, holding up her dolls as she made them fly. She'd avoid me like I was invisible, focusing entirely on whatever magical place her mind had conjured. Other times, she'd be swinging around her house, twirling in time to the record player she'd sneaked on, the volume creeping higher with every spin.

Even back then, she was different. While I was learning the world's rules from my dad, she created her own. The memories flicker like an old film reel, warm and imperfect. I wonder now if she saw me as more than just a background figure in her world.

I sip my coffee again, the steam curling upward like the questions I can't bring myself to ask. But then the darkness comes swirling in like it always does when you look back too long. The memory of my dad sitting across from me, his jaw tight and his voice cutting sharper than any blade.

"Aspen Farms? What kind of fool idea is that? You'll fail before you even start," he'd say, slamming his palm on the table for emphasis. The words weren't just harsh. They were final. Like he'd already decided my dream wasn't worth the effort. I can still feel the sting of his spit hitting my face as he yelled, as if his anger was a physical force meant to push me down. He uprooted the plan before it had a chance to grow, but that didn't stop me from leaving. I packed my things, squared my shoulders, and walked out that door, determined to prove him wrong.

For a while, I did. Aspen Farms was more than a plan—it was a reality—my reality.

Until the flood came, the memory of it is like a storm cloud, heavy and relentless. The rushing water stole everything I'd worked for, every hope I'd planted in the soil. And now, here I am, back in Havenwood, sipping coffee and pretending the cracks in my foundation don't still ache. Pretending I don't hear my dad's voice in my head, even now, questioning if I'll ever be more than the boy he once shouted down.

I glance at him now, sitting across from me. The years have softened him in ways I never noticed before—his shoulders slouch just slightly, his hands move slower, and his voice carries a weight. He's smaller and quieter, but his presence still commands the room, like gravity bends around him.

I love him. I always have, even when it hurts. Even when his words left scars, I didn't know how to heal. I've spent my entire life chasing his approval, twisting myself into shapes I thought he'd admire. But I can't do it anymore. I can't keep being a version of myself that only exists in his shadow.

I look at him again, and something shifts. The anger, pain, and years of resentment dissolve, falling away like leaves in autumn. Because at this moment, I don't just see my father. I see myself. The stubbornness, the relentless drive, the impossible expectations—we're cut from the same cloth, even when I tried so hard to believe we weren't.

"Listen, Emmett." I hear him choking on his words. I straighten, trying to regain control of my spiral. "I've been . . . I've been feeling it for a while now with my health. It isn't what it used to be. I don't have that strength and energy I once did, and the truth is, it is harder for me to keep up."

I sit up straighter, my stomach still tightening. "What do you mean?" I ask, even though I think I know. He gives me a small, tired smile. Oh, Dad. Even at this moment, he will try to be strong.

"I am not saying that I am on death's door, kid. I am slowing down, though. I mean, hell, being both the last chairman of the town board and the mayor . . . a man is doomed to be exhausted." He sips his coffee again, swallowing hard. "But I have to admit it now. I can't keep doing it all." His voice is soft but firm. "Especially with the ole Fall Festival rearing its head. I have done it for years, but I need you to grab the bull by the horns."

I choke on the last sip of coffee. Coughing, I set the mug down a little too hard. "I am sorry, what?" I stare at him with mixed emotions. "The entire festival, alone?"

Dad nods his head, his expression serious. "I trust you. You haven't been involved much since you've been gone, but this town needs you now. I need you."

That last part rings in my ears: *I need you.*

He needs *me.* I don't know what to say. I've always respected his work for the town—everyone does—but I have never imagined him asking me to step in like this. I thought I would just come back, help out here and there. But take over this project entirely? God knows what else he may tack on.

"I have never run something like this before. I mean, sure, the logistics can't be too hard compared to Aspen Farm to Table, but still—" I protest and hear my own words, but my heart already knows I will do it for him.

He reaches across the island and places his rough hand on mine. "Listen, you will be fine. You have the skills for it, even if you aren't sure yet. The vendors, the planning, all of it—it's in good hands with you."

"I'll do it." I didn't take my eyes off my old man's hand on mine. The years have surely aged them, but his youth and playfulness still reside. I swallow my emotions because it is too early to feel these things, and this coffee isn't improving my mood.

"One more thing." He taps my hand.

Now what? "What's that?" I pull back, trying to balance myself as I get up off my stool, b-lining for the bagels.

"I want Ophelia involved this year," he says, his voice firm, like he's been thinking about this for a while. I blink and look up, thrown off completely and surprised by the sudden statement.

"Ophelia? Why?"

He smirks at me like I should know better than to ask. "Because it's time, Emmett."

I frown, not understanding. "Time for what?"

Dad sighs, setting his mug down. "You don't see it, do you? That girl has been locked away in that house ever since Willie passed. Sure, her teahouse keeps her busy, but it's not the same. She's pulled away from everyone, from the town. That's not what Willie wanted for her."

He pauses, the weight of unspoken words hanging in the air. "You know, before he passed, Willie asked me to keep an eye on her. Said he worried she'd bury herself in that house and forget there's a whole world outside those walls. He made me promise, Emmett. He didn't want her just to exist—he wanted her to live. To be part of this town, part of something bigger."

I shift, his words absorbing slowly.

"I can't do it alone anymore," Dad continued, his voice softer now. "I need your help. You've got a way with people—maybe you can get through to her. The festival is a good excuse. It's small, it's manageable, but it's something. A step back into the community."

I stare at him, unsure what to say.

"She's got too much heart to let it go to waste," Dad says, his eyes meeting mine. "Willie saw that. I see it. And I think you do, too."

I sit there, processing. *Ophelia* . . . "You are serious about this, aren't you?" It wasn't a question. I knew he was.

But in true Ron fashion, he looks at me with that knowing expression that always makes me feel like a kid caught sneaking out.

"Yeah," I say, my voice steady, though I wasn't sure if I was trying to convince him or myself.

"Go see her. Talk to her. You might be surprised at what she can bring to the table."

I nod, the weight of another task settling squarely on my shoulders. This wasn't how I imagined my return to Haven-wood. But if it's what Dad wants—and maybe the town, too—I'll find a way to make it happen. Even if it means figuring out Ophelia in the process. I have a feeling this would be an adventure with very polarizing outcomes.

Dad leans back in his chair, his gaze following me.

"Oh, something else," he says casually, but his tone gives him away. "I'm moving you to 'as needed' at the post office."

What now? I raise a brow. "You're cutting my hours?"

"Let's just call it an adjustment," he shrugs. The comment hangs in the air, not accusatory but pointed enough to make me pause. He didn't press further. He gives me a look that says he's not blind to the wheels turning in my head.

"Right," I say, more to myself than him. But he can see there is more on my mind.

Tilting his head, his eyes narrow slightly. "You're still living off the farm sale, right?"

The question hits like a dart, dead-on and sharp. My jaw tightens, and I shove my hands into my pockets. "What's that got to do with anything?"

"It's got to do with everything," he says, his voice steady but firm. "You sold that land to chase something bigger, but here you are, back in Havenwood, still chasing. You need to figure out what the hell you're actually running after, son."

"I sold that land because I had no choice. That was my dream—that's what I was running after." My voice wavers as I study him, searching for something in his expression. "Or maybe you forgot who called me home," I spit out. The words taste bitter even as I say them. My tone lacks conviction, and his silence only makes it worse. "I just need time," I whisper, the admission hanging in the stillness between us.

"You've had time," he counters. "What you need is a plan. That money won't last forever, and if this festival thing isn't part of whatever dream you've been building in your head, you'd better start thinking about what is."

I hate how easily he cut to the truth like he'd been sitting on it, waiting for the right moment to strike. I shift uncomfortably, my gaze fixes on the floor. "I know, Dad. I'm working on it."

"Well," he says, leaning back in his chair with a smirk creeping onto his face. "One thing's for sure—you're not cut out for delivering mail. Never were."

The comment caught me off guard, and he grins.

"Remember when you delivered Mrs. Hensley's package to the wrong house?" he says, chuckling. "Old man Harvick opened it up, thought she'd sent him flowers as a peace offering for the feud over the fence line. You damn near started a town scandal."

I couldn't help but laugh, shaking my head. "That was years ago, Dad. And you know Harvick's a nosy old coot who would've opened it no matter where it got delivered."

"Maybe," he says with a shrug. "But you'd still make a lousy mailman."

"Good thing I'm not planning on making a career out of it," I shoot back, though my voice lacks the confidence I want.

He gives me a pointed look, his amusement softening into something more serious. "Exactly. So, figure out what you are planning, Emmett. Because Havenwood's a nice place to settle down."

I didn't have a response, at least not one I was ready to say out loud. So, I nod and mutter something about heading out. The weight of his words sitting squarely on my chest as I leave the room. Dad had a way of making me think harder than I wanted to. And maybe that was the problem. For all the plans I thought I'd made, I wasn't sure I really had any at all.

Chapter Five

OPHELIA

The crisp autumn air greets me as I push open the back door, arms full with bins of decorations I'd pulled from the storage room.

Impending doom sits in my chest at the mess the room has become, and I mentally move it up on my to-do list. It's the perfect early morning for decorating. Clouds roll lazily across the sky, and the trees around Havenwood were ablaze in fiery shades of orange, red, and gold as Indiana did it best. My teahouse nestles among them, a little plain—but not for long.

I set the bins down on the porch steps and breathe in the scent of fallen leaves and distant woodsmoke. Like the woods exhaled after a long summer, the air carried a hint of earthiness. A steaming cup of chai sits on the porch railing, untouched since I made it, but its cinnamon aroma is just as comforting as the warm knit scarf around my neck.

Let's do this. I begin with the door, pulling a grapevine wreath wrapped in twigs, tiny pumpkins, and faux leaves out of the first bin. I hang it on the hook of the front door, adjusting and fluffing the orange ribbon. I step back—it hangs perfectly center. *Wow, it already feels more like autumn.*

I move on to the wooden rocking chairs set off to the side,

covering them with cushions embroidered with golden leaves and plaid patterns. A cozy throw drapes across one of the chairs, inviting anyone who might stroll by to sit and relax.

I couldn't help my cheesy smile. It was all coming together. I dug elbow-deep into the second-to-last bin, searching for my favorite lanterns. I place one on each step, adding a sprig of faux berries and small gourds around their bases. When evening comes, the glow of the candles will cast a warm shadow across the porch. I can't wait to see it.

"Oh, hello, dear friend," I murmur, a small giggle escaping as I pull out the scarecrow I'd affectionately named Mr. Patches years ago. His faded overalls and lopsided grin still offer warmth and familiarity. Propping him up by the flower box, I use my apron to dust him off. The dust catches in my nose as I sneeze.

Ope. The flower box is overgrown with the last of my summer herbs. I clip a few rosemary sprigs and tuck them into my apron pocket. *They will taste fantastic in tonight's biscuits.*

I add "cleaning the flower box" to my mental to-do list. Finally, it's time for the finishing touches—my favorite thing— the garland. Made of handmade felt leaves in every autumn hue, it always took some wrangling to hang just right around the porch railing. When I finish, I'm taken aback by how a few festive decorations strung together could transform a space. It's perfect.

As I set the extra thumbtacks in the bin, my hand brushes against something unexpected. I frown, pulling out an old book with a leather cover—*The Gardener's Almanac.* I hadn't seen this in years. The corners were long and frayed, the spine cracked, and the leather worn. I flip through. The pages ice-cold from being in storage. The smell of the book took me back.

Not to somewhere I want to go. A letter falls out as I shut it and return it to the bin. I pocket the paper absentmindedly, popping the lids on the bins and maneuvering back into the home. I'm a little behind—the working hours are about to begin. I take the letter from my pocket as I head upstairs, my fingers tracing its worn and soft edges. Step by step, the creaks of the old wood echo in the house's stillness, each sound settling deeper into the quiet.

My bedroom feels like a sanctuary when I enter, its familiar warmth wrapping around me with such familiarity— a safe haven.

The air is rich with the scent of lavender sachets tucked in drawers and the faint sweetness of gingersnap cookies from the candle on my nightstand. I move to the dresser by my favorite window, which catches the morning light just right. It's cluttered with pieces of me: a collection of tiny bear figurines that have followed me through every season of my life. Among them—scattered are vintage ink pens whose smooth barrels still remember the feel of my words. A few clippings from my favorite baking magazine sit in a loose pile, recipes I promised myself I'd try but never have. And there's my geode—the one I cracked open years ago, its crystalline heart glinting in hues of yellow and white. It sits in a gold frame, angled perfectly so the sun dances through it, casting soft rainbows across the walls.

I set the letter down carefully, intending to add it to the papers that await my attention—another task I've avoided for too long. But as I let it go, the sunlight streams through the window, catching the paper just right. The ink shimmers—a familiar green that pulls me back instantly. My heart sinks, a heaviness settling over me as if the letter itself knows more than I'm ready to confront.

No . . . I hold the letter tighter, my palms suddenly damp.
Dad's handwriting.

I haven't seen it in so long, but it's unmistakable—his loops and swirls, the ink always a shade of green I could never quite find anywhere else. My legs feel weak, but I secure myself on the edge of my bed. I grab a pillow, placing it on my lap, as I begin to unfold the letter, hands trembling.

I read. It's a letter I know by heart, yet every word still cuts deeply.

> Baby Dolly,
> Do not forget you are more than just aprons and teacups. Go live a little—NO, go live a lotta bit! You are an angel, kiddo. Someone will be lucky to make you their wife one day. Make sure they can find you.
> Love you a billion green M+Ms,
> Dad

My vision blurs, hot tears streaming down my face as I read the last part four more times. The words are both comforting and heartbreaking. How did he always know the right things to say? I clutch the small silver cylinder hanging from the chain around my neck. It's a piece of him I carry with me everywhere.

Kissing it gently, I whisper, "I love you, Dad. I wish you were here with me . . . root beer floats and sunsets . . ."

I glance back at the letter before carefully folding it as if closing it might keep the memory intact and protect it somehow. Slowly, I set it aside, its weight lingering in my chest.

It's as if I can hear him repeating those words, urging me to live beyond the confines of this house, to find something more. I just . . . I don't know how.

I am cutting it dangerously close. Time is slipping away, and I have yet to do anything I need to ensure a smooth opening. I look around, tears still blurring my sight. I swallow my emotions and get up, pulling open the drawers of my heavy dresser. I snake my hand inside, feeling for a familiar comfort.

Aha! My cream cable knit cardigan. I slip into the bathroom, managing a quick shower. I stand in front of the full-length mirror, leaning against the wall behind my bedroom door. My fingers fumble with the wooden buttons of my oversized cardigan. The soft knit, always healing, hangs loosely around me, draping over my body like a shield.

I pause for a moment, looking at my reflection. My long brown hair, the ends still damp, falls over my shoulder in waves. It frames my face, highlighting my round cheeks and the fullness of my lips, now glossy with a tinted lip oil.

I tuck a strand behind my ear, my fingers grazing the soft skin of my neck. There is something different in my eyes today —a weariness I can't quite shake. Maybe it's the dark circles under them, a reminder of another restless night spent overthinking. I let my gaze drift lower, taking in the rest of me— the soft curves, the fullness I always try to hide beneath layers of cozy clothes. The cardigan, as familiar as the four walls of my home, hugs my body, making me feel safe, like always.

But today, as I inspect myself, something tugs at me. A question. A flicker of something I can't quite name. *Live a lotta bit.* I take a deep breath, smoothing the fabric over my hips, unsettling thoughts creeping up. I turn away from the mirror, but that image of me—of the me I could be—stays with me, lingering in the quiet.

I am downstairs just in time for the knock on the door. I can see reflections of shadows behind the stained glass. I glance at the clock on the wall—thirty minutes—I am thirty minutes behind!

I feel it in the pit of my stomach. As I open the door, my heart sinks. A small group of people are waiting outside— regulars, except for one or two. Their faces don't show frustration or impatience. Instead, they smile warmly as if my absence isn't a big deal.

"Good morning, Ophelia!" They all say in unison.

"We figured you were just having one of those mornings. We all get them," Morgan says from the back.

I nod, forcing a smile, "You could absolutely say that, darling."

I usher them all in. My heart races as I flip the sign to "Walk-ins are welcome." Pulling up the notebook and cash case, I hurry behind the main counter. People begin filing in, chatting amongst themselves, completely at ease, but all I can think about is how far behind I was. The kettle isn't even on. Worst of all, there are no fresh baked goods.

My mind is whirling. I hadn't made anything this morning. Not a single scone or muffin. What am I going to serve them? I glance at the clock. Every minute feels like an hour. I see Morgan going to the counter, a plant in her arms.

"Here you go!" she says. "They were going to toss this one out yesterday, but all he needs is some water." She hands me a string of slightly shriveled pearls.

I beam with anticipation, eager to get the plant healthy again. I set it behind me on the shelf where the others are, adjusting the plant light to reach the new addition.

Morgan works at *The Tattered Basket* and often brings me sick or slightly dying plants to revive. This happened for months after she caught me in the dumpster trying to save a dehydrated peacc lily.

Hey, don't judge. She's also Emmett's sister, but I try to forget that part.

"Can I get an Earl Grey to go?" Morgan asks, smiling at my enthusiasm about the plant.

"Of course! Coming right up, lovebug!" I reply, but it isn't . . . nothing is coming up.

The water isn't even boiling. I grab the teapot, fill it, and set it on the stove while mentally running through what I can serve with the tea. Nothing. I had nothing.

How could I not have managed time better? A tap on the

backdoor has me perk up. I move the curtain from the small window and peek out. Wren, the homeschool co-op leader.

Shit. I run to the fridge, grab the day-old bakery items in the containers, and rush to the door.

"Here!" I say cheerily.

"Oh, you are the *best!*" she says above the stack of containers. She winks and blows me a kiss, giggling as she walks to her car and yells, "Thank you!"

"Always," I yell back. At least the kiddos will have some goodies, right?

A bead of sweat trickles down my neck—I can't do this alone. My hands shake as I pick up the phone, dialing Florence's number. She answers after the first ring.

"Ophelia! What's up?" Her voice sounds surprised.

"I—I need you to come over," I blurt out, keeping my voice low as I glance around the busy room. "I haven't baked anything, the teahouse is packed, and I'm. . . I'm drowning over here."

There is a pause. Florence never hesitates with these things, but I can feel the shock coming through the line.

"You need me to come over?" she repeats, her voice soft, like she can't believe what she heard.

When I look around, the walls feel like they are moving in on me. "Yes," I whisper, "Please, Flo, I have never been this far behind. I–I need you." My sight begins to blur, and tears threaten to escape.

"I'm on my way," she says, concern heavy in her tone.

I hung up and return to the group, who still hasn't noticed the rising chaos behind the counter. They sit, sipping their drinks—or would be if I could get the tea made—chatting, laughing. But all I can sense is the clock's ticking, the kettle taking too long to boil, and the empty glass display case staring back at me, mocking me with its emptiness.

Florence arrives quicker than I expect, her eyes wide when she walks in. She takes one look at me, her face full of concern. "Ophelia, what happened? You never ask for help. Are you okay?"

I let her words sit with me for a moment. Do I mention the letter this morning?

"I don't know," I admit, rushing to make the first round of teas. "I just lost track of time this morning. I feel off."

Florence jumps in to tidy up the counter, her hands moving with precision.

"This isn't like you," she says gently. "Maybe you are taking on too much."

I don't respond. I don't want to think about what that might mean. Instead, I focus on the task, trying to catch up with the day that had somehow gotten away from me. Florence moves behind me, tidying up the space without a word. Her quiet presence, usually comforting, made me a bit uneasy.

I try to ignore the voice in my head—the one that told me she might be right. Maybe I am pushing myself too hard.

No . . . I've never needed anyone. Not really. When things break, I fix them. When people doubt me, I prove them wrong. It's pride that kept me going. Just the simple fact that I couldn't count on anyone else. I think back to that first winter after Dad passed, the silence in the house heavier than any snowfall. The holidays were looming, and the thought of spending them alone made my chest ache.

So, I decided I wouldn't.

That December, I organized the first Havenwood Christmas Charity Drive. It started small—a few gift boxes and a flyer in the teahouse's window. People brought donations of toys, coats, and canned goods. I spent hours sorting everything, wrapping gifts in cheerful paper, and delivering them to families needing extra cheer.

By the second year, it wasn't just me. The town got involved. Local businesses donated, kids made cards, and even the high school choir sang carols as we handed out the gifts.

But even as it grew, I stayed behind the scenes, ensuring everything ran smoothly. It wasn't about recognition—it never was.

I sip my tea and smile faintly, remembering the joy of those moments—the way Mrs. Kline cried when she opened the door to find a brand-new coat for her grandson or how the Jones twins grinned ear to ear when they unwrapped their matching sleds. Those memories warm me more than the tea ever could.

And it's not just Christmas. Every fall, I quietly donate to the school's art program, enough to cover the year's supplies. Every spring, I bake dozens of cookies for the town clean-up volunteers, sneaking extra lemon bars to the kids who work the hardest. Every day, the teahouse is my way of giving back —a place for people to gather, feel at home, and find comfort in their busy lives.

I glance at the counter where the community board hangs, its edges curling with age. Flyers for upcoming bake sales, lost-and-found notices, and thank-you notes from patrons clutter its surface. It's a small thing, but it's mine—it is a quiet way to keep people connected. I think about how often people have told me, *"You should ask for help more, Ophelia."*

The sentiment is kind, but it misses the point. I don't need help. I never have. When the roof leaked last spring, I patched it myself. When the supply chain issues meant I couldn't get my usual tea blends, I improvised with herbs from my garden. And when the septic tank backed up in the middle of the night last summer . . . well, I learned more about plumbing than I ever wanted to.

I've handled it all and done it on my own. That's just who I am. But today, as the tea cools in my mug and the shadows lengthen across the room, I wonder if I've built something too strong, too self-reliant. As much as they've protected me, my walls have kept me from letting anyone else in. The thought lingers, uncomfortable but persistent.

"You've always been so organized, Ophelia," Florence

murmurs, the soft sound of her voice barely rising above the quiet hum of the teapot. "You don't need to do everything by yourself. You don't have to be perfect all the time."

I wince, feeling the sting of her words. But I didn't know how to stop. How could I stop?

This teahouse—this life—was the one thing that grounded me. If I lost control of it, what would I have left?

I glance at Florence, the weight of her quiet understanding almost too much to bear. She is right. This isn't like me. But how could I slow down when everything was in motion? The store is more bustling than it has been in months. I still hadn't finished the list of things I had promised to get done. And every time I thought about the idea of slowing down, I feel like I'm failing.

I shake my head, trying to push the feelings down. "I'm fine," I say, but my voice is too soft, too unsure to convince anyone, least of all myself.

Florence doesn't push any further. She simply gives me a knowing look—a look that tells me she is waiting for me to come to terms with it on my own, but the doubt is already settling in.

I focus back on the task, pretending the weight in my chest isn't there. Pretending the fear of being overwhelmed isn't creeping up on me. I'm not ready to admit it. Not yet. But deep down, I know Florence is right. And I don't know how long I can keep pretending everything is okay.

My chest tightens as I move toward the counter, my hands fumbling with the delicate tea leaves. As the minutes pass, I realize that the truth lingers no matter how much I try to drown it out. I am failing, and the worst part is that I am not sure how to fix it.

Florence saved me. This morning's rush of customers is now on their way with cinnamon raisin bagels and pumpkin bread, some opting for tea to-go. The afternoon rush is now cycling in. Florence steps up, making sourdough turkey and avocado sandwiches, heavy on the mayo and pepper jack cheese, for a few locals she knows will sneak in asking.

Her attention to detail amazes me, though. She has watched me run this place solo for years.

"Go sit down and have a sandwich," Florence says firmly, placing a plate in my hands. "I'll handle the rest of your shift. But seriously, go eat." She twirls around, grabs a bottle of water from the fridge, and presses it into the crook of my arm. "And hydrate too, missy," she adds with a playful wink.

I peer around the room. Only a few customers linger, quietly sipping their tea, absorbed in their books or laptops. The usual hustle and bustle has calmed, leaving the space feeling peaceful. My eyes drift to the cozy corner, where my favorite chair sits empty, practically calling my name. Without a word, I make my way over and sink into the plush seat, its softness instantly comforting me.

The tension I'd been holding all morning begins to ease as I stare at the plate in my hands. It's already early afternoon, and this will be the first bites of food I've eaten all day. After finishing my sandwich's last bite, I hand the plate back to Florence. She gives me a quick smile, already setting the kitchen back to its usual organized state. I need a moment to myself, so I hurry upstairs, escaping the constant buzz of my inner thoughts for just a minute.

I lean against the doorframe of my room, taking a deep breath, trying to center myself. I watch as Poe darts back and forth in the hallways upstairs, finally loafing in a spot that was in the sun to bask away.

I stand at the window, my fingers brushing against the lace curtains I'd sewn with Mom years ago. The stillness of the room holds me in place. My eyes drift to the oak tree in the backyard, its branches swaying gently in the breeze. I thought of Dad's letter, his words returning to my mind during quiet moments like this. I swallow hard, my chest tightening.

Was I doing enough? That question had haunted me since

his letter arrived the year I had been on the verge of selling the teahouse. I even met with a buyer, walking them through the house, trying to explain what it meant to me without letting on how much it terrified me to let it go. And to be clear, I didn't want to let it go.

I just . . . I need to restart and build something new, but I can't. I can't welcome the change. It terrifies me.

I decide to head back down the stairs, careful down each step. Below, I hear voices from the kitchen—Florence and someone else . . .

I pause, listening—Emmett.

As I round the corner, Florence looks like a deer in head-lights. "Emmett and I were just talking about the decorations."

I step into the kitchen, avoiding Emmett's eyes but unable to stop my gaze from drifting back to his boots. "That, in fact, is what kept me busy all morning, so forgive me for the unstable events today. The decorations paid off, though," I reply, trying to sound casual.

"My sister loves it when you decorate," Emmett says, glancing around the room. "She prefers coming here to study and says she likes to write in her journal. Something about the 'aesthetically pleasing ambiance.'"

I chuckle. "She always brings me plants from the general store, you know, the ones they can't sell. We call them 'test subjects.' I try to bring them back to life with new soil, light, and a little extra love."

Morgan is the opposite of Emmett. So kind, warm, and a true delight. He was . . . cold, dull, and not a delight. We drift to the main room, finding comfy chairs. Florence drinks the last few sips of her tea and stands up, stretching.

"I will pop this in the sink, sweet girl," she says.

I shake my head as she walks by, briefly touching my shoulder.

Emmett shifts in his chair, and I sense a hint of hesitation. His emotions are not always easy to read.

"You must really be enjoying that bagel," I tease lightly.

He chuckles deeply, trying to wipe cream cheese from his mustache and beard.

"Did you like the sandwich yesterday?" I ask.

He chokes on a piece of the bagel as he hit his chest, "Sure, Mossgrove, but it was a little wet," he grins.

Whatever.

Florence gracefully reenters, "I got to head out real quick. The shop is closed, but Jessica says there is a line around the block. Those silly folk can't read the damn sign." She points at me. "Come here. Let me show you the setup for the evening rush."

I jump up, not wanting to keep her waiting. I stick my tongue out at Emmett, "You aren't even the least bit kind, are you?"

He perks up, not expecting my childish remark, but honestly, neither was I. I walk into the kitchen expecting a spread of food for the evening rush, except I see Florence with her arms crossed. "Listen, you are closing early. I don't know what happened this morning, but you need time. You need a moment. Your entire aura today is off, and it breaks my heart."

The bluntness surprises me. I clutch the necklace around my neck, pressing the cylinder to my lips.

Florence's eyes follow the movement. "Oh, my angel, I get it. No explanation needed." She kisses my cheek and hugs me tightly before whispering, "You've built something beautiful here, but even the strongest trees need the wind to help them grow tall." She nods toward Emmett as she steps back, her words settling deep in my chest. With a wink, she leaves.

Suddenly, I am acutely aware of how quiet the room has become. Emmett and I are alone, and the weight of that realization makes me nervous. I peek at the clock—it's nearly closing time anyway.

I offer a sheepish smile and sink into the chair again, feeling a little awkward.

"You aren't kind either, little lady." He returns my childish act earlier with his tongue sticking out, then winks.

Gross. I have no words, or rather, just no words for Emmett. I am also not the best at wrapping up things or insinuating that someone needs to leave, as I very much need to do.

"How's the ole hunk of metal out there treating you? Did you run it like I said you should?" He gives me a stern look.

No, I didn't.

"You didn't, did you?" He gives me a head tilt, those hazel eyes staring at me with daggers ready to strike. Can he read my mind?

Penguins. Peanuts. Hot chocolate. You are the rudest, weirdest, smelliest man in Havenwood. Get out of my house.

"Careful, Mossgrove, your brain isn't meant to think that hard." He kicks my boots, and I kick his knee.

He hunches over in pain.

"Get out." My words are flat, and I suppress a laugh as I reach for any ounce of confidence in my body, but all I am being met with is doom and laughter. What a variety.

"What is your issue with assaulting mailmen?" He gets up, and that is when it erupts.

I would have rather the doom be what spills over, but no . . . bubbles and bubbles of pure belly laughter come spitting out of me. I am holding my knees as all the laughter releases.

I am mad. I've have gone mad.

Between Dad's letter this morning and now this, I am done. I am simply and utterly done. *Take me, Lord, my time has come.* Just let me pack my herbal teas and my cups. Are there kettles in heaven? I can't stop—not until I peer up, tears flooding my eyes, to find Emmett standing before me, stone-cold and pale.

His eyes are the only thing alive with emotion, and they tell me he's confused.

"Yep, you really are the crazy lady in the woods, with your little herbs and your . . . whatever the hell those are," he says, pointing to my green cowboy boots.

"You can diss my tea, you can make fun of my bird's nest hair, but you, Emmett Sterling, will not get away with dissing my Tony Lamas." I get up, a magazine I've sneakily rolled up in hand, ready to crack this idiot on the head.

Why is it that with him, my anxiety is smothered? Before I can manage a single playful-ish swing, Emmett grabs my wrist. I grunt in shock, his rough hands firm and steady as they hold me.

He bends my arm down, his voice low as he says, "You aren't capable of hurting me, little lady. So, try all you might —it's pointless." His grip tightens ever so slightly, and I glare at him.

"You're awfully confident for someone who underestimates me," I say, my voice softer now.

His smirk returns, but it doesn't quite reach his hazel eyes. "Maybe. Or maybe I just know you better than you think." The air between us feels heavier than it should, charged with something I'm not entirely comfortable with. I force a small laugh, trying to break the tension, and toss the magazine onto the chair.

"Next time, you won't see it coming," I quip, but even I can hear the forced lightness in my tone.

"Looking forward to it," he replies, his eyes traveling over my shoulders. "Go start your truck, Mossgrove. It seriously needs it," he adds, his voice carrying that same quiet intensity. As he turns and walks away, I can't control my eyes. I watch him like a hawk, my pulse racing.

For the first time, I'm not entirely sure if I want to challenge him again—or if I'm afraid of what might happen if I do.

Chapter Six

EMMETT

"Here to disappoint me again?" Gage looks down at me, a smile buds.

"Oh shut up, and get my usual." I sit down on the stool across from him, and he presents me with my drink and, of course, more bullshit.

"Negroni for the homie," he grins.

He hasn't let up on me about my drink of choice in years. Sure, whiskey sounds nice, but something about the classic profile of a Negroni does it for me. The wafting cigarette smoke chokes my lungs, but Gage is still ripping into me about my drink. Typical.

"You won't get any women with a drink like that," he shoots at me.

I smirk, unfazed. "I have no need for any of these women." I twirl my finger around. I didn't need to look. I already knew that Patty is dancing with too many men, Lauren is eating steak and fries while entertaining Mr. Jacobs, and a few out-of-towners were thinking about how to get lucky.

I didn't fit in here, but that never stopped me from coming.

Gage was my childhood best friend, and there wasn't a Saturday that went by that I didn't come to support him.

I could be nice . . . sometimes. I take a few chips and dip them in queso. I stop myself before ordering steak and fries. I have enough leftovers to last me a few months, but nothing could get between me and my queso. It was practically a Saturday routine at this point—one my uniform wasn't too happy about. A headache forms behind my eyes, and the pressure to get Ophelia to agree to the festival is weighing on me. She really hasn't returned since her father passed, and honestly, that was about when she stopped coming out altogether. I miss seeing her around town, even if I was too stuck in my ways to admit it in any other way than mentally.

I sip my drink, my muscles relaxing as if on cue. I tune back into reality.

"Speaking of which," Gage continues, "There has been a pretty fine lady that comes around every evening to pick up a to-go order, but she never stays."

Interesting. No one in their right mind orders to go from a bar, much less *The Barkeeps*.

I loved my steak and fries because they were free, courtesy of, again, my childhood best friend.

A woman with deep burgundy hair emerges from the back, a to-go bag in hand as she rounds the corner and sets it on the counter. Her appearance is rough— apron greasy, hair pulled up in a messy bun, and face mask hanging from her ear. She looks up at Gage, who is still going on about this mystery woman.

"She'll be here any minute, so stop gushing over her and get back to work." She winks and disappears back into the kitchen. I peek at my watch. I should be leaving, but curiosity has me sold on this lady. I know almost everyone in this town, and none of them fit this character.

I lean back on the bar stool, trying not to take too deep a

breath as someone chain-smokes behind me. The music dips low, a steady thrum echoing in my chest.

Heavy footsteps drown out the melody, drawing my attention. I scan the room and spot the source—a figure draped in a velvet green hooded cloak. My gaze shifts to Gage, whose smile spreads like a secret unfolding.

This must be her.

This mystery woman steps forward, reaching for the bag on the counter. In its place, she sets a parchment bag tied neatly with a ribbon. Strange. The exchange happens in silence—no words, no acknowledgment. She turns, her cloak sweeping dramatically around her ankles, revealing light green Tony Lamas.

Mossgrove. A chuckle tickles my throat, but I bite it back. I press my lips together, suppressing my amusement and the flicker of curiosity that tightens in my chest. The chime of her departure pulls me back, and I exhale the breath I didn't realize I was holding—only to meet Gage's sharp stare.

"You know her, don't you?" he asks.

I shrug, deflecting with ease. "I know everyone in this town. My dad's the mayor, and I'm the mailman. Not many secrets here, bud." He isn't convinced, but the burgundy-haired cook appears from the kitchen before he can press further. She grins, grabbing the parchment bag.

"Thank goodness. I love her cookies," she says, cradling the bag. "She's such a sweetie pie."

I fight to hold my tongue, but it slips. "Ophelia does make some good cookies," I reply, offering my kindest smile. The cook perks up, her face lighting with shared enthusiasm.

"She and her dad—an old friend of mine—always came here. Spicy wings were their favorite," she says with a wistful smile. "After her dad passed, I kept feeding her. Makes me feel better knowing she's eating. That one doesn't talk much, though. And now, I only see her every so often. Usually, that thrift store owner . . . uh . . . " She looks to the ceiling, fishing for the name.

"Florence?" I offer.

Her smile widens. "Yes! Florence. She usually picks up the wings for her." With that, she hugs the bag and vanishes back into the kitchen.

So, it was a secret—or at least something Ophelia would hate for me to know. I drain the last of my drink and give Gage a curt nod. If this was how she kept her dad's memory alive, who was I to make light of it? Still, I can't get past those boots. I wouldn't use this against her, not ever. But it gave me a glimpse of a side of her I hadn't seen before.

Ophelia had always seemed soft, but this was something else—fragile in a way that felt too precious for me to claim, and I wasn't in the business of tainting anything pure like her.

Chapter Seven

OPHELIA

I wipe my spicy, herb-oiled fingers on the napkin beside me, savoring every bite of these wings. Gilmore Girls reruns play in the background, my eyes stinging and bloodshot from hours of watching. Somehow, that lands me in the bathtub at 4 a.m., a book in hand, pretending I'm fine. Pretending I'm not avoiding my feelings.

But who am I kidding? That rich honey-vanilla scent could only belong to one person, even if I try to convince myself otherwise. The only man I know—six feet of smugness —who sips Negronis and somehow smells like a cookie.

Nevermind. Nevermind. Nevermind. I won't sit here, soaking in bubbles, thinking about him. Not Emmett. Not again. Not ever.

His words echo in my head anyway, uninvited. *"Maybe I just know you better than you think."*

My cheeks flush, heat crawling up my neck. Hmm . . . maybe. I force my attention back to my book, restarting the same chapter for the fourth time, determined to focus. No wandering thoughts of tall cowboys with perfectly rough hands, drinking Negronis, their hair catching the light like— ugh, stop.

He is weird. And mean. And . . . *Emmett Sterling.*

He's not going to hijack my delirium at 4 a.m. I need to sleep.

With a sigh, I step out of the bath, gripping the counter for balance. The cold air prickles my skin, and goosebumps rise as shadows from the cracked door dance across me. For a fleeting second, I picture him standing there—looming, watching. My cheeks flush deeper. What is wrong with me? I wrap my robe tightly, shame curling in the pit of my stomach.

Back in my room, I slide under the covers, careful not to disturb the warm, purring bundle of fur curled beside me. Tomorrow is Sunday, and Mom will be visiting. Plenty to do. I rest my hand on Poe's belly. His soft purring grounding me as sleep tugs me under.

Goodnight, world. Goodnight, Emmett.

Early mornings like this, with the sunlight just beginning to stretch across the countertops, are when I feel most like myself.

The world is still, the town asleep, and for these few precious moments, it's just me and the hum of my baking routine. I lean over the counter, carefully splitting a vanilla bean pod down its center, the tiny black seeds clinging to the knife's edge.

The scent is intoxicating—sweet, floral, warm. It's a smell that always feels like home, like comfort wrapped in nostalgia. I scrape the seeds into a mixing bowl, watching the flecks disappear. Flour puffs softly into the air as I measure it, adding it to the bowl with a pinch of salt.

The sticky and fragrant dough comes together with my hands. I press it gently into a circle on the floured counter, using my pastry cutter to slice it into perfect triangles. There's something so soothing about the process, each step familiar and grounding.

I place the scones on a baking sheet lined with parchment paper and brush their tops with cream, sprinkling a dusting of sugar for a touch of sparkle. Sliding them into the preheated oven, I close the door and breathe deeply, anticipating the comforting aroma that will soon fill the kitchen.

While the scones bake, I take a moment to tidy up, the sound of running water and the clink of dishes keeping me anchored in the present. This is where I feel most calm—my hands busy, my mind quiet. The oven timer dings, and I grab my mitts, carefully pulling the tray out.

The scones are golden and slightly crisp on the edges, their soft centers promising warmth and sweetness. I set them on the cooling rack and admire my work, the kitchen bathes in the soft glow of accomplishment. A soft knock at the kitchen door draws my attention.

"Morning, sweetheart," my mom says, stepping inside with a warm smile. She's wearing her favorite sweater, the one she's had for years, and her eyes light up when she spots the scones. "Are those what I think they are?"

"Vanilla bean," I reply, grabbing the kettle to prepare the tea. She walks over to the counter, hovering just close enough to the cooling rack that I know she's resisting the urge to grab one.

"You've outdone yourself, Ophelia. They look perfect."

I smile softly, setting the kettle on the stove and measuring loose-leaf tea into the pot. "Let them cool a little, Mom. You'll burn your mouth like last time."

She laughs, leaning against the counter. "Can you blame me? Your scones are worth the risk."

The kettle begins to whistle, and I pour the steaming water over the tea leaves, watching as the amber liquid swirls and deepens. The aroma of bergamot and citrus blends with the lingering sweetness of vanilla in the air, creating a symphony of scents that feels like a hug. I carry the teapot and two mismatched mugs to the table, my mom pulling out a chair. She eyes the cooling scones, her fingers tapping impatiently on the table.

I grab a small plate and place two scones on it, sliding them across the table toward her. "Here. Just don't say I didn't warn you."

She eagerly takes one, breaking it open and releasing a soft plume of steam. The first bite earns a satisfied hum, and her eyes close as she savors the taste.

"Perfect as always," Mom exclaims, bouncing on her toes. Sundays are my recipe-testing days, and Mom is my most enthusiastic taste tester—well, except for that one time I attempted mille-feuilles and accidentally used spoiled cream. That disaster taught me to smell-check everything.

Mom polishes off the scone and reaches for another, her eyes wide with delight. "Honey, I'm not kidding—these are simply perfection." Her voice brims with genuine giddiness, though she tries to play it cool.

I smile as I arrange the aster cuttings she'd brought in brown jars, their purple petals vibrant against the earthy glass. "I'm glad you love them. I was thinking of adding them to this week's menu," I say, catching her sneaking a crumb to Poe, the ever-hungry cat. His tail twitches in delight as he rubs against her legs. I chuckle softly—he'd do anything for food.

The lightness of the moment carries us through hours spent cleaning the storage room, an overwhelming task I've avoided for far too long. Mom's presence makes it bearable, her determination cutting through my hesitation. Every time I tried tackling it alone, I froze—paralyzed by its sheer weight. But with her help, the impossible becomes manageable.

When we finally finish, I step back, marveling at the transformation. "Wow," I breathe, the word barely audible as I took in the now-organized space. Mom lingers by a corner of the room, her fingers brushing over a small piece of floral wallpaper that clung stubbornly to the wall.

Her voice softens as she says, "I remember when this was your bedroom. You'd sit here every night, playing your guitar, humming as you studied. Your dad and I would tiptoe to the door, skipping that creaky floorboard, to listen to you sing." Her eyes met mine, and I saw the emotion swell before tears begin to spill.

I cross the room and hug her tightly, my chest aching at the rare sight of her breaking. She'd always been the glue—the unshakable strength in our family—but I knew how hard it was for her to be here. Every corner of this house was a reminder of my dad. Chester Mossgrove, her knight in shining armor, her lifeline, and my dad.

I've locked away the master bedroom—the room they'd shared—on the second floor. I couldn't bring myself to go in, even two years later. I didn't know if I ever would.

"Ophelia?" Mom's voice pulls me from my thoughts, her hand warm against my cheek.

"S-sorry," I stammer, forcing a small smile. "I was just thinking about those times."

She nods, her emotions retreating as quickly as they have surfaced. "I think I'll head into town, grab a few things from *The Tattered Basket,* and maybe stop by to see Flo. I'll be back around lunch."

I offer another weak smile as she leaves, the screen door clicking shut behind her. My hands shake as I fill the kettle, pouring the hot water into a mug. I stir it absentmindedly, the tea infuser clinking against the spoon. My stomach growls, and I reach for a scone, only for it to slip from my trembling fingers. It tumbles to the floor in slow motion.

My shoulder knocks into the counter as I bend to pick it up, sending the teacup crashing down. Scalding liquid splashes over me, and I yelp as the hot water sears my skin.

The cup shatters at my feet, a kaleidoscope of porcelain shards.

I freeze, staring at the wreckage. The burn throbs, but the pain is nothing compared to the storm brewing inside me. Tears blur my vision, and a sob tears through me—deep and raw, ripping apart the fragile walls I'd built around my heart.

I sink to the floor, my hands shaking as the tears come in uncontrollable waves. I cry for my dad, for the dreams I'd buried, for the life I'd hidden from behind these walls. I cry for the scone and the teacup and for the girl I used to be.

The air inside feels suffocating. I stumble to my feet, clutching my chest as I bolt out the back door. The fresh air hit me like a tidal wave, but I still couldn't breathe.

Pacing in the yard, I look at the sky, begging for calm.

"Ophelia?" His voice cuts through my spiral, grounding me.

Emmett stood at the edge of the house, his eyes darting from my tear-streaked face to the burn on my chest. I can't speak. I can't move. All I can do is cry.

"Hey, hey," he says softly, stepping closer. "Are you okay?"

His words break something loose, and before I know it, he guides me back inside. He doesn't question the mess in the kitchen. He just shields me from it as he leads me to a chair.

"Sit," he orders gently. I obey, too drained to argue. He presses a cool, damp cloth against my burn, his touch surprisingly tender.

"Just breathe," he says.

I close my eyes, his steady presence calming the storm inside me.

"I don't know what happened," he says after a long silence. "But whatever it was, you're strong, Ophelia. You're stronger than you think."

My throat tightens, and all I can manage is a shaky, "Thank you."

A faint smile tugs at his lips as he hands me a paper bag. "I know it's early, but they reheat well," he says, the smell of spicy wings wafting up.

"Emmett," I murmur, looking up at him. His expression was different—gentler, almost vulnerable.

"I'm serious," he says, brushing a strand of hair from my face. "You're one tough woman, Mossgrove." Then, with a teasing grin, he adds, "Don't get used to deliveries from a good-looking man, though. It'll start costing you."

For the first time that day, I laugh. As he leaves, I return to the kitchen to clean up the mess, only to find it spotless.

Emmett Sterling—annoying, mysterious, and . . . unexpectedly kind.

Chapter Eight

EMMETT

It's been two weeks since my unexpected exchange with Ophelia.

Spicy wings and a good laugh did wonders because, ever since, things around her have become . . . interesting.

Every day this week, she'd orchestrated little performances on her front porch as if to feign busyness whenever my route brought me to her house.

On Monday, she was dusting the chairs on her porch, even though they were spotless.

Tuesday, she was fluffing the already perfectly arranged wreath on her door. By Wednesday, she was craning her neck to stare at something in the distance—something imaginary, I'd realized after following her gaze and finding absolutely nothing.

But that wasn't all. Ophelia had been out and about lately.

The first time was at the *Tattered Basket*. I caught a glimpse of her with her arms full of potted plants, a soft smile gracing her lips. Despite her calm exterior, I could see the fear flickering in her eyes as she navigated the checkout line.

I kept my distance, primarily out of shock. Seeing her in public felt like watching a butterfly emerge from its cocoon.

This wasn't for anyone else. It was for her. The plants weren't what gave it away—it was the quiet relief on her face when she passed through the checkout with her bags and receipt. She looked around as if to see if anyone had witnessed her small victory.

You did it, I thought to myself.

And she really had. The next time I saw her was early morning before sunrise. As I set a package on Mr. Jacobs's porch, I turn to find her walking down the cobblestone street. Her usual boots swapped out for questionably colored running shoes, paired with leggings that hugged her legs.

My gaze travels upward, expecting a baggy shirt. Instead, I find a black sports bra with mesh cutouts teasing her skin under the dim streetlights. Her soft curves move with each step, and for a moment, I am completely still.

Wow. She is . . . breathtaking.

But it isn't just her appearance that catches me off guard; it's how different this version of Ophelia felt. She glances back at me as I wrestle with my thoughts and flashes a wide smile.

"Watch out, Sterling!" she yells as I walk straight into the side of my truck. The bruise on my knee isn't the only thing that lingers after that encounter.

The third time, she cornered me at *The Cabinet of Curiosities*. I was sifting through the antique rows, hunting for a specific item my mom had tasked me with, when I saw her standing there. Her long hair was braided over her shoulder, and her layered skirt brushed the floor. The silver buckle on her belt glinted in the light, and, of course, those green boots completed the look.

Her lips part slightly as if she hadn't expected to see me but wasn't upset about it either. "Emmett," she says softly, her voice curling around my name like it was something precious. She fidgets with her hands, her thumbs twisting nervously.

God, I loved the way she says my name.

"Ophelia," I murmur, and her cheeks flush pink. For a

moment, we stood there, the silence humming with unspoken words. Then she shifts past me in the narrow aisle, her back brushing against my front. Every nerve in my body lights up at the contact. I walk out of the shop empty-handed but with my mind full of . . . well . . . alot.

Sitting in my truck outside her teahouse this Thursday evening, I wonder what kind of performance she'd treat me to today.

The wind howled through Havenwood, tugging at my jacket as I grab the final letters and a package labeled for her. I even triple-checked. The weight of the envelope in my hand feels oddly significant as I approach her porch, determined not to glance up.

But then I did, and my breath hitches.

She stands a few feet away, holding two steaming mugs. Her expression is a mix of emotions, each carefully guarded, but her voice is soft when she says, "Come in?"

I hesitate.

"Please?" she adds, and that one word cracks something inside me.

"Yeah, sure." I never did like keeping a lady waiting. The warmth of the teahouse envelopes me as I step inside. The air is thick with the comforting scents of chai, baked goods, and something floral. My stomach betrays me with a growl, and I pray she doesn't hear it. Not now.

She leads me to a pair of wingback chairs by the fire, navigating the maze of mismatched furniture like it was second nature. I sit awkwardly, the dainty mug in my hands looking ridiculously small. As I sip it, chai's spiced warmth melts some of the tension in my chest.

"How was your route today?" she asks, setting the package on her lap.

"It's been busy. I guess even on an as-needed schedule, I can't get away from this dreadful mail season," I reply, grateful for the distraction.

She smiles, unwrapping the package to reveal a beautifully illustrated journal. I watch her take notes in the journal. "Turns out writing my feelings isn't as cliché as I thought," she admits with a sigh.

I perk up. "I've noticed you've been out more lately. *The Tattered Basket*, your walks, Florence's shop—"

She cut me off with a nod. "Exposure therapy," she says, her voice barely above a whisper. "For my anxiety."

I set down my cup and take her hands in mine. Her startled jump making me pause. "I told you, Ophelia. You're stronger than you think."

Her fingers are still in mine, and she meets my gaze.

"I have some errands tomorrow," she says hesitantly. "Do you think . . . you could go with me?"

She wants me to go with her? *Hell yes.* "Mossgrove, are you asking me to be your chauffeur?"

She giggles, and the sound melts every defense I have left.

"Absolutely," I say, standing and grinning down at her. "I'll be here. But don't get too used to a handsome cowboy running errands for you."

Her lips quirk into a playful smirk. "Handsome? You're far from it." We both know she is lying. And as I walk out, already looking forward to tomorrow, I can't help but chuckle.

Me? On a date with the feisty herbalist. *Finally.*

Chapter Nine

OPHELIA

I wake slowly, soaking in the familiar weight of Poe stretched across my legs. He is warm, purring softly as he absorbs the morning sun shining from the window on the bed. For all his trouble, he can be a real sweetheart when he wants to. I smile, eyes half-closed, basking in the soft glow filtering through my bedroom window.

It's one of those mornings where everything feels right—until my mind drifts to today's plan. *Meet Emmett for errands.* Just thinking of his name sends a rush of heat through my cheeks. My heart skips a beat, and I bury my face in the pillow, groaning softly.

I'm way too excited for this, way too nervous, but I can't help it. It's been ages since I've felt this kind of anticipation about going out with someone. Is this a date?

Late last night, in a moment of pure, confused emotions, I decided not to open the tea house today. It's a little reckless of me, but I want to get ready, to feel confident before seeing him. Outfits and hairstyles spun in my mind all night, keeping me awake far longer than I should've been.

I finally drag my body out of bed, gently patting Poe on the head as I slide my feet from under the covers and place them on the cold hardwood floor. He cracks open his eye, uninterested in anything that doesn't involve more sleep. Typical.

As I shuffle toward the bathroom, the sight of toilet paper shredded and strewn across the floor greets me. I sigh, glaring at Poe, who is now happily lounging in the sun like the chaos gremlin he is. "Poe, I thought we were friends," I mutter.

He purrs in response, clearly unbothered by his overnight destruction. I shove the mess to the side with my foot, deciding to deal with it later. Looking into the mirror, I take a deep breath and say, "Today will be a good day."

And it is. I can feel it.

I go through my morning routine with a mix of excitement and nerves buzzing through me. After a shower and some mental pep talks, I stand in front of my closet, picking out my outfit for the day. I settle on a fitted black dress—simple, but it feels right for today. I throw on an oversized sweater and buckle belt to complete the look, pairing it all with my trusty green boots.

My hair, neatly braided, rests over my shoulder, and I look at my reflection one last time. Butterflies stir in my stomach, but I remind myself that I am fine—and capable.

Downstairs, I feed Poe, who gives me a half-interested glance before turning his attention to his food bowl. I decide to skip breakfast, my nerves too jittery for anything more than a cup of tea. As I sip from my favorite mug, the minutes stretch longer and longer.

My meeting with Emmett isn't until later, but the anticipation is already getting to me. Just as I'm about to settle in, my phone buzzes.

A text:

Can you meet earlier?

I blink, staring at my cell phone in confusion. Another text follows.

> Emmett. Sorry, this is Emmett. Flo just gave me your number. I am here at her shop getting something for my mom still, damn thing. If you want to meet at the flower shop in the next few minutes, I am free . . .

My heart races. Meet now? Already? I glance at the clock and then at my reflection in the glass panel of my china hutch. I whisper to myself, "Live a lotta bit." I don't care how many times I need to repeat these words to myself. I can do this.

With a deep breath, I reply:

> Hey Emmett, that sounds great. I'll be there shortly.

I grab my tote bag, give Poe a quick kiss on the head—dodging his playful swat—and head out the door. The comforting autumn air greets me as I step onto the porch, carrying the earthy scent of fallen leaves and the promise of change. My boots crunch on the gravel as I stroll down the small path leading to the main road. A small smile creeps across my face, and I close my eyes briefly, breathing deeply.

It feels like a good omen, and I let myself savor the quiet beauty of the day as I make my way toward the heart of Havenwood, passing the *Tattered Basket*.

The sun hangs low in the sky, casting long shadows across the cobblestone streets, the golden hues of the morning still clinging to the town. It's peaceful today—no hurry, no rush, just the soft bustle of small-town life. People greet each other with easy smiles and waves as I pass, and for the first time in a long while, I find myself returning each wave, a sense of connection flowing through me that's both foreign and comforting at once.

Cheyenne, the librarian, stands outside and arranges a sign in front of the door. She looks up as I approach. Her face lights up when she sees me. "Ophelia, darling! How are you today?"

"I'm well, Chey," I reply, smiling at her warmth. "The weather's beautiful."

"It sure is—just the right kind of day for a walk. Don't be a stranger, dear," she says with a wink, her dainty hands return to the sign.

"I won't be," I assure her, feeling the tinge of hope in my voice. *Maybe this isn't so bad.* I cut through the parking lot. As I continued on, I notice a few more familiar faces. Tom from the newer hardware store gave me a wave, and I wave back, my heart lightening with each small interaction.

Something is comforting about these moments, these simple exchanges with people I've known all my life. I round the corner of the main street and stop in front of *The Barkeeps*, drawn by the inviting aroma of something delicious from the kitchen. I glance through the open window and catch sight of Rosa, the cook and my dad's good friend from high school. Her broad shoulders are hunched over the counter, chopping vegetables, her dark eyes focused but warm. She looks up when she notices me standing there and gives a nod of recognition.

"Ophelia!" she calls out, her usual gruff tone softened by a friendly smile. "I hadn't seen you in a few days. I miss my cookies!"

I chuckle, feeling a little embarrassed but mostly glad to see her. "I should bring some by for you all soon. I promise."

"You should," Rosa agrees with a wink.

I wave as I continue down the street. I'm not just the reclusive baker and herbalist anymore . . . I think. I'm starting to become part of the fabric of this town again, one small gesture at a time. It's only a few more steps to the floral shop, and as I approach, I spot Emmett standing near the front display, leaning down to examine a bucket of flowers. His brow is furrowed in concentration, a look that's almost endearing in its intensity.

There's something about how he carries himself—like he's trying to figure out the world around him but hasn't quite found all the answers yet. It's. . . well, it's endearing.

I roll my eyes at myself, unsure why I'm even thinking about him this way. I am not going to fall for Emmett Sterling. Not now. Not ever. But even as I try to convince myself, I feel that pull—the one that's always there, even when I ignore it.

I think of the days when I was younger, back when the world felt simpler, even if I didn't understand it at the time. My mind drifts to those summer afternoons when I'd be in the backyard, twirling and dancing in the flower fields, the soft petals brushing against my bare feet. The house was quiet, but I somehow knew that Emmett was watching.

He was always there—somewhere on the edges of my life, his eyes on me as I sang quietly to myself or pretended to be lost in the world of my own imagination. I never liked to acknowledge it, never wanted to admit that I could feel his gaze. It made me self-conscious, even though I tried not to show it. There were times I'd catch him, his figure framed by the window, his presence so close yet far away.

He was always the quiet one, the brooding one, the one who kept his distance. But I was always aware of him. I remembered how he lingered in the background during family dinners—his father and mine talking about business or the town, while Emmett would just watch.

He never spoke much, but I knew he was listening. Always watching, always observing. It made me nervous how he seemed to take everything in, but he never seemed to care enough to talk to me. I'd catch him sometimes, his eyes on me as I played with my dolls or sat under the big oak tree with my sketchbook, but I never dared to speak to him. It was like we were two separate worlds—his so full of expectations and mine so full of escape.

He had his place in town, always seen but never truly known. And I had mine, a quiet corner tucked away in the back of Havenwood, far from everyone else's chaos. But it wasn't until the year my father passed that things changed.

I remember the day like it was yesterday. The house was full of people, of sorrow, and yet it felt empty all the same. I'd retreated to my room, as I always did when I needed to escape. That was when I heard the knock on the door. I wasn't expecting anyone. And when I opened it, there he was. Emmett Sterling—standing in the doorway, looking like he had all the answers, but his eyes were filled with uncertainty.

For the first time, he wasn't standing at a distance. He was there, right in front of me.

"I'm sorry about your dad," he'd said, his voice low, unsure. It was the first time he'd ever spoken to me, really spoken to me, outside of the fleeting glances and the silence we shared as children. His words caught me off guard, and for a moment, I didn't know how to respond. I had grown so used to keeping to myself that I forgot how to connect with others.

And yet, there he was, breaking the silence in a strange but needed way. He wasn't just the boy who watched me from the shadows anymore. He was here, standing in front of me, a part of my life in a way he hadn't been before. I couldn't even remember what I said to him—some awkward words, no doubt—but I remember how we both stood there, unsure of what came next.

The moment lingered, heavy and unfamiliar. But then he left . . . and now . . . he is back—here in front of me.

I snap back to reality, avoiding the pull to roll my eyes at the betrayal of my mind. He stands up and looks around, his gaze landing on me. His eyes flicker momentarily before a smile tugs at the corner of his lips.

"Those are surely beautiful, aren't they?" I acknowledge the flowers he was just intensely staring at.

He dreamily whispers, "You are."

I feel my cheeks flame as the words hang between us. He clears his throat quickly, stumbling over his following words.

"I mean, yes, yes, they are."

We both stand there for an awkward moment. Emmett looks at me again, breaking the tension with a deep, rumbling laugh. I laugh, too, more out of relief than anything.

"Apologies, but yes, these are beautiful, aren't they?" He picks up a small bouquet of wildflower cuttings and smiles.

"These would look amazing in the tea house." I nod, grateful for the change in subject, as we head inside the shop. The floral shop is small but cozy, filled with the scent of fresh blooms and soil. Emmett hands the bouquet to the florist, and I can't help but notice how comfortable he is here, as if he's been there a hundred times before.

Seeing him so at ease in a flower shop is strange when I've always thought of him as the rugged, get-things-done type. As we wait for the bouquet to be wrapped, I steal a glance at him. He's standing by the counter, hands in his pockets, looking down at the flowers like they have a deeper meaning.

I feel a flutter in my chest again, realizing how easy it is to be around him. How natural this feels. As I stand there next to Emmett, I can't help but wonder if this is how it starts.

Quietly, gently, with a bouquet of flowers and a smile.

Chapter Ten

EMMETT

Ophelia is breathtaking. Lit by the sun cascading in from the window, she is practically glowing.

Though, it is so much more than that.

The way she moves, gently brushing her fingers over petals like she's sharing a secret with each bloom, the way her eyes brighten at the sight of dahlias—everything about her feels so delicate and yet, at the same time, so mysterious. She belongs here, among the flowers and beauty the universe created.

I watch her quietly, trying to take it all in without being obvious.

Damn. She is just perfect. I could watch her for hours, days even, and still find something new to admire. As she circles back toward the dahlias again, for what feels like the tenth time, I can't help but smile.

"Dahlias catch your eye, Mossgrove?" I murmur.

She looks up. "They are just . . . so beautiful," she whispers.

As I stood there, Lisa, the shop owner, caught my eye. I gesture for a pen, and she slips me a small sticky notepad and a pencil. My fingers move quickly across the paper as I scribble down a request:

24 dahlia stems sent to Ophelia Mossgrove,
0518 Wood End Drive, the tea house.

Lisa grins as she reads the note, then winks at me, mouthing the word, "Note?"

I squint, confused for a second before I understand what she means.

"Do you want to add a note?" she whispers, nudging the pencil back toward me.

I glance over at Ophelia to make sure she's still busy, then quickly take the pencil back, writing:

In every bloom, I see a reflection of you—delicate, resilient, and endlessly captivating. Like these petals, your presence brings color and light to the quiet corners of Havenwood. Know that you are so cherished.

I pause mid-sentence, my pen hovering above the page. The words I've already written say everything I need them to —for now. Ophelia's voice gently breaks through my focus. She approaches the counter with a hesitant grace, her hands fidgeting as if searching for purpose.

"Thank you for coming with me today, Emmett," she says softly. Her gaze falters, and her voice wavers. "I haven't been in here since Dad's f-funeral . . ." Her eyes cloud with emotion, and without thinking, I step closer.

"You're welcome, muffin," I say, keeping my tone light. "But don't think you're getting off scot-free. I expect payment —just not in the usual currency."

Her eyes widen, the flush creeping up her cheeks. "W-what do you mean?"

"Cookies," I reply with a chuckle.

She narrows her eyes, but a smile tugs at her lips. "Oh, whatever. Tell me what kind, and I'll bake them tomorrow. But don't get used to it, Emmett. I'm a busy woman," she declares with a dramatic twirl before heading for the door.

I watch her go, a grin tugging at my lips. That was my cue to wrap things up.

"Lisa, do you mind having Luke take these to Ophelia's this afternoon?" I hand her back the wildflowers Ophelia picked out. "I've got a few other things I need to do, and I don't want them to get damaged."

Lisa nods, "Of course."

I hurry to catch up with the speedy little lady ahead of me.

"Those flowers are beautiful. I could spend all day in that place," she says.

I nod, glancing at my watch. I'm not trying to ignore her, but a thought crosses my mind: "Have you eaten yet?"

She shakes her head, the familiar shyness creeping back into her expression. Seeing that vulnerability stirs something bold in me. Without overthinking, I reach for her hand. She stiffens at first, but then her fingers slowly relax into mine, and the warmth of her hand sends a rush through me.

"Come on, let's grab some subs," I say, gently squeezing her hand. We stroll to the sandwich shop, order our meals, and settle into a cozy booth by the window. The small talk flows easily between us, as though this were a ritual we've shared a thousand times before.

Ophelia starts telling me about her plans to make a pectin-free jam, her enthusiasm lighting up her face.

I raise an eyebrow, cutting her off. "Okay, but . . . what's pectin?"

She laughs, the kind of laugh that makes her eyes crinkle at the corners, and launches into an explanation. I listen, though the science of it mostly goes over my head.

Then, with impeccable timing, I can't resist: "Sounds like your kind of . . . jam." It's a terrible dad joke, but it lands.

She bursts out laughing so hard she nearly spits out her soda. That sets me off, and soon, we're laughing louder than anyone else in the shop. For a moment, everything else fades —the festival, the expectations weighing on me, even the constant pressure from my dad.

In this booth, with Ophelia's laughter echoing in my ears, the world feels simple, trekkable.

"We really need to work on your jokes, Emmett," she snorts. I'm already diving deep into the recesses of my brain, searching for another joke that might actually land and stay, when her voice cuts through my thoughts.

"So . . . that's why I thought maybe I could . . . try," she says, her eyes locking on mine, brimming with hope.

Shit. I missed something. "Sorry, little lady," I say, flashing her a sheepish grin. "I was too busy trying to impress you with my next masterpiece, but the old brain hit a wall." Her gaze stays steady, and I soften. "What were you saying?" I ask, my tone gentler now, a silent prayer that she won't mind repeating herself.

I watch as emotions flicker across her face, each one tugging at her in a different direction. Finally, she starts, her voice soft and deliberate. "I-I've been thinking about the festival," she says, taking a small sip of her drink.

My heart skips a beat. The festival. "What about it, muffin?" I ask, keeping my tone casual, though my curiosity is anything but.

"Well . . ." She hesitates, her fingers tracing the edge of the table. "Maybe I could have a booth this year. Something small, but . . ." She trails off, her gaze flicking to mine.

I'm hanging onto every word and pause until she finally finishes. "I'd need help. A lot of help."

It takes a moment for her words to click, and then it hits me—Ophelia Mossgrove is asking for my help. Again.

"Done," I say firmly, maybe a little too quickly, but I manage to keep my excitement in check.

"What?" Her head tilts, and she looks at me like I've just grown a second head.

"I'll help you, little lady," I reply with a grin. "No sweat off my back. Besides, getting bossed around by someone as feisty as you might even be fun." I throw in a wink for good measure, and for a moment, I swear I catch the tiniest hint of a smile.

Chapter Eleven

OPHELIA

"Thank you," I murmur shyly, handing the cashier my card. My eyes drop to the haul spread out before me. I did some serious damage in *The Tattered Basket* today, but oddly, it feels incredible.

Groceries, new books, supplies to restock my tea recipes, and more. It's the kind of indulgence I rarely allow myself, and for once, I don't feel guilty.

Emmett steps closer, the warmth of his presence brushing against me. I freeze as he leans in, his breath grazing my ear. "You did great," he whispers.

Chills spread across my neck, his words carrying a weight I hadn't expected. He doesn't move away, and something inside me stirs—a soft ache I can't quite name. I glance down, catching sight of his hand dangling just inches from mine. My heart skips as I stare, so lost in thought that I don't notice the cashier handing my card back.

Emmett reaches for it, his brows knitting with concern as he glances at me. I let out a nervous chuckle, trying to shake the conflict warring in my head. My heart urges me to grab his hand, but my brain holds me back. What is wrong with me?

Without a word, he scoops up the bags, effortlessly balancing them on one arm. I stand there, still staring at his hand like it holds all the answers I'll ever need.

His fingers twitch, and he clears his throat. "Little lady?"

I can't meet his eyes, too embarrassed to respond. But this is Emmett Sterling—the ever-surprising cowboy who never seems to miss a thing.

Following my gaze, he lets out a deep, rumbly chuckle before slipping his hand into mine. "It don't bite, muffin," he says, his voice laced with humor.

And just like that, my heart skips again, but I don't want it to stop this time.

Emmett pulls the truck into my driveway, parking with the ease of someone who's done it a hundred times. *He has.* He hops out before I can reach for the door handle, rounding the truck and opening it for me. "Stay put," he says, his drawl low but firm. "I've got the bags."

I don't argue. Watching him gather every single one of the shopping bags in one swoop is a sight to behold. His confidence, the way his arms flex as he hoists the weight—it's infuriatingly attractive. I unlock the door, step inside as Emmett follows, and lug the bags into my kitchen.

"Where do you want these, little lady?" he asks, setting them on the counter.

"Right there is fine," I say, already starting to unpack. But Emmett doesn't leave.

Instead, he shrugs out of his jacket, rolls up his sleeves, and begins unpacking alongside me.

"You don't have to—" I start, but he cuts me off with a pointed look.

"Not letting you do this alone," he says, pulling out a carton of eggs and placing them in the fridge. We fall into an easy rhythm. I organize, and he hands things to me or puts them away himself. It's quiet for a while, but then he pulls out the books I bought.

"Well, well, what do we have here?" he drawls, flipping through the stack. "*The Lost Apothecary* sounds fancy. Ooh, *Love in the Vineyard*—sounds romantic. And . . ." He stops, holding up the third book with a slow, mischievous grin. "*A Touch of Midnight*? Let me guess, not about gardening."

My cheeks flame. "Put that down, Emmett!" I snatch it from his hands, stuffing it into a drawer.

He laughs, a deep, rumbling sound that fills the kitchen. "Didn't peg you for a smut reader, Mossgrove. This day just keeps getting better."

"Shut up and finish putting the cereal away," I grumble, trying to hide my embarrassment. But he doesn't let it go. Even as he moves back to the counter, he throws me teasing looks over his shoulder, a mischievous glint in his eyes.

"I'll try not to judge you *too* much," he says, clearly enjoying how he's flustered me. "You've got a whole secret life hidden, huh?"

"Oh, please," I grumble, crossing my arms. "You're impossible."

He smiles, leaning against the counter casually. "That's what they all say."

A beat of silence passes, the teasing undercurrent still swirling in the air, and for a moment, I forget that we're supposed to be pretending this is just another casual day. This banter between us feels different now—almost as if it's its own kind of language, something that's only ours. My heart stirs unexpectedly, and I quickly turn to distract myself with the tea kettle, trying to hide how my pulse quickened.

"Alright, alright," I say, changing the subject. "You want tea? Or are you just going to keep making fun of me?"

"Tea sounds good," he replies, still grinning. "And maybe you can teach me about *Touch of Midnight* over it."

I roll my eyes, but the smile I can't suppress gives me away. "Just finish unpacking the groceries, Emmett."

He chuckles again, but there's a softness this time as if he knows exactly what he's doing. "Alright, little lady."

The evening air crept inside from the poorly insulated windows. I curl up on the couch. The lamp's soft glow beside me casts a warm light across the room. Just out of reach, my heated blanket calls my name, but I ignore it. I knew these books always made me heated . . .

The tea has long since been finished, and now, I'm nursing my embarrassment with a book in my lap. The very one Emmett teased me about earlier—*A Touch of Midnight*.

The cover, dark and mysterious, looks innocent enough, but the contents? Well, let's just say it wasn't related at all. I glance at the page, my fingers tracing the lines of text, but my mind drifts back to Emmett's teasing smile and how he'd kept throwing me those playful glances. I feel my cheeks warm again just thinking about it.

I try to focus on the book in my hands, but all I can think of is how he'd laughed when I'd snatched the book away and how his eyes seemed to linger just a little too long when he looked at me. I flip the page, the words beginning to blur together as I sink further into my teaughts.

Had he been flirting with me? No, that was ridiculous.

Emmett was messing with me like he always did. Still, something about the way he'd looked at me today . . .

I exhale sharply, shaking my head. "Get a grip, Ophelia," I mutter, trying to get back into the book, but it's useless. I feel the heat of my blush refuses to fade. As I settle into the quiet, I hear a soft ding-dong at the door.

My heart skips. Confused, I set the book down and rise from my cozy spot to answer the door. Who could it be this late? When I open the box, a small delivery box sits on the step, with a bouquet of the most beautiful flowers I've ever seen. My breath catches, and I crouch down to pick them up, a slip of paper tucked neatly under the string holding the bouquet together.

I blink at the paper, my pulse already racing as I unfold it.

I see a reflection of you in every bloom—delicate, resilient, and endlessly captivating. Like these petals, your presence brings color and light to the quiet corners of Havenwood. Know that you are so cherished. - Emmett

I stand there frozen for a moment, the note warm in my hands, and my cheeks flush even deeper. I can't believe it. I can't even breathe properly.

He—Emmett—he sent me flowers?

Suddenly, my embarrassment from earlier felt insignificant. The teasing, the way he looked at me—everything starts to make sense in a new light. The playful banter and teasing smiles weren't just about getting under my skin.

Was it? I glance at the flowers again, my fingers brushing the delicate petals.

Emmett . . . likes me?

The thought is enough to make my heart race and my chest tight. I swallow, unsure of what to make of it. I peek at the note again as though it might change somehow, but it doesn't. The handwriting is neat, and the words still stand, clear and simple. I close the door slowly, holding the flowers close to me like some precious secret, my mind racing with questions.

Did Emmett mean it? Was it just a gesture? I feel my heart flutter unsteadily as I sit back on the couch, the flowers beside me and the note's weight in my hand. I can't help but smile while feeling that familiar rush of uncertainty.

Maybe he had meant it. Maybe this was something more than just his usual teasing. As my fingers lightly touched the petals again, I let out a shaky breath, wondering what this meant for us. If anything. What if I let myself care for him? What if I open up, let him see me, and it all falls apart?

I'm no stranger to disappointment, rejection, and the quiet ache of being misunderstood. Being in a relationship . . . it's just as scary as the thought of being exposed in public, of no longer being hidden behind the walls of my teahouse. That was already something I was working on.

I swallow hard, the familiar fear creeping in. A relationship would mean vulnerability—letting someone into the space I've carefully curated for myself. It would mean trusting someone with my heart, which I haven't been able to do in so long.

What if I let him in, and he sees all the cracks and ways I'm not enough? What if, after all this time, I still can't break free from my fears? I let out a slow breath, closing my eyes for a moment. A part of me wants to run—to take these flowers and hide them away like I do everything else. But then I think of Emmett, his teasing smile, the way he looked at me today, and for a brief moment, I wonder if maybe I could allow myself to be seen.

But then the fear sets in again, louder this time. What if he doesn't like what he finds? I tuck the note into my pocket, my heart heavy with uncertainty. I stare at the flowers once more, the bright colors so different from the muted tones of my life. *You are going to be okay.*

Chapter Twelve

EMMETT

The next day, I find myself back at Ophelia's place. Her teahouse is quiet this evening, sunlight streaming through the windows and pooling onto the polished wooden floors.

I feel my muscles relax. A long day at work is now behind me. The cozy charm of the place matches her perfectly—warm, welcoming, and entirely her own.

I grab a seat off to the side, close enough to keep an eye on her but far enough to stay out of her way. She's moving behind the counter, all soft focus and small smiles as she pours tea and chats with her regulars. Her laugh, scent, and warmth cling to me like the morning dew.

The door to the back room creaks open, and a woman I do not recognize steps in. I sit up a little straighter.

"I'll make this quick," the lady says, her voice low and kind. "I just wanted to say I'm proud of your progress. It's clear you've been doing a lot of reflection."

Her therapist?

Ophelia sets down a tray of teacups, her brow furrowed slightly. "Thanks. I've been trying. Really, I have."

"You have. But . . ." The therapist hesitates. "We need to

talk about the teahouse again. It's still holding you back in some ways. You've told me how it ties into your sense of identity, but sometimes . . . holding on too tightly can prevent us from growing."

Ophelia doesn't respond right away, and the silence feels heavy, even from where I'm sitting. "You think I should sell it," she says finally, her voice soft but steady.

"I think you should reflect on it. Just reflect," the therapist says. "Think about whether staying here is what you truly want or if it's simply what feels safe. We talked about it! You can still have a cafe, or even a bakery, or another teahouse, but these four walls suffocate you."

I look down, pretending to focus on my phone, but my stomach twists.

Sell the teahouse?

I can't imagine Havenwood without Ophelia's teahouse, without her filling this space with her quiet magic. The therapist gives Ophelia's arm a reassuring pat before leaving through the back door.

I glance up, and Ophelia is already moving, slipping seamlessly into her role as the town's comforter and caretaker. She takes orders, pours tea, and smiles like nothing is weighing on her. But I know better now. She brings a tray to a table of two older women and laughs at something they say. Her laugh is as light as it always is, but there's a tightness in her shoulders I didn't notice before. She moves to the counter, chatting with customers as she works, and I watch her, wondering how much of her is hidden beneath that smile.

It's late before she makes her way to my table, a pot of tea in hand. "You were early today," she says, pouring me a cup.

"Couldn't stay away," I say with a grin, though my mind is still turning over what I heard.

She sits across from me, smoothing her apron. "I'm glad you came. I was hoping you'd stick around until closing. We need to go over a few things for the festival."

"Of course," I say immediately. "Anything you need."

Her smile softens, and she nods. "Thank you, Emmett."

The afternoon passes in a blur of tea and chatter. I help her with small things—restocking shelves, moving boxes—but mostly, I watch. Watch how she interacts with her customers and lights up when someone compliments her baking. It's clear she loves this place, but now, knowing what I do, I can't stop wondering if it's enough for her. As the last customer leaves, I roll up my sleeves and head to the sink.

"You're not closing alone," I say when she starts to protest. "I'll do the dishes."

She doesn't argue. She hands me a dish towel with a small smile. We work side by side, the clink of porcelain and the hum of the sink filling the quiet. It's peaceful. Almost too peaceful.

Then, out of nowhere, she says, "I know you heard that."

I glance at her, my hands pausing mid-scrub. She's focused on drying a plate, her expression carefully neutral.

"I don't know what you mean," I lie, though it's not very convincing.

She lets out a soft laugh, shaking her head. "You're not exactly subtle, Sterling. You think I didn't see you trying to blend into the wallpaper earlier?"

Caught me. I set the plate down. "I wasn't trying to eavesdrop." I was a little bit, but c'mon . . .

"I know," she says, finally looking at me. There's no anger in her eyes, just . . . something else. "It's fine. Really. It's just —" she hesitates, then shrugs. "It's complicated."

"Complicated how?" I ask, my voice softer now.

She shakes her head again, brushing me off. "Don't worry about it."

But I do worry. More than I want to admit. Because the thought of her letting go of this place—of her—makes my chest ache in ways I can't explain. I had no jokes, witty banter, or drive to be funny. I just felt . . . empty.

Later, I sit across from her, my elbows resting on the surface as I lean forward, trying to focus on what she's saying. Ophelia is talking about the festival, asking questions about booth placement and vendor fees, but her words are muffled in my mind, drowned out by everything I overheard earlier.

She asks, and I answer. The energy has shifted, and it doesn't take a genius to see that. Why would she even consider selling this place? Her teahouse isn't just a building. It's a cornerstone of Havenwood. The thought of it being anything other than hers doesn't sit right with me. I watch as she jots something down in her notebook, her brow furrowing in concentration, and my chest tightens.

My mind drifts to Aspen Farms—the life I tried to build after leaving Havenwood. I'd poured every ounce into that land, believing it was my ticket to freedom and success. But then the flood came, and with it, everything I'd worked for washed away. It wasn't just a financial blow—it was personal. The farm had been my dream. Losing it felt like losing a piece of myself.

Is that how she feels now?

"Emmett?" Her soft voice pulls me from my thoughts. She's looking at me, her head tilted, her pen poised over the notebook.

"Sorry," I say quickly, sitting up straighter. "What was that?"

"I asked if you thought setting up near the florist would be a good spot," she repeats, her tone patient but curious.

"No, maybe closer to the town hall," I answer, though I'm not really thinking about the festival. My eyes wander to the shelves lined with jars of loose-leaf tea, the mismatched chairs, and the faint smell of cinnamon and bergamot lingering in the air. This place is her.

She closes the notebook, her movements slow and deliberate, and leans back in her chair. "You're distracted," she says, not accusing, just observing.

I let out a breath, deciding not to dodge it this time. "Yeah. I guess I am."

Her gaze drops to the table, and for a moment, the only sound is the faint creak of the wooden floor as the building settles. Her shoulders are tense, but she doesn't look surprised.

"I don't get it, Ophelia," I say, leaning forward again. "This is your home. Your life. Why would you want to just uproot it?"

She's quiet for a long time, her fingers tracing the edge of her notebook. When she finally speaks, her voice is steady but soft. "Because it's not just a home, Emmett. It's a weight. A beautiful one, but still a weight."

I blink, not expecting that answer. "A weight?"

She nods, her eyes distant. "This house . . . it's where I grew up. Where I spent countless hours with my dad, learning to bake, blend tea, and take care of people. It's also where I watched him grow weaker. Where I sat by his side as he took his last breath. Every corner of this place is steeped in beautiful and painful memories. And as much as I love it . . . it's suffocating me."

Her words hit me like a freight train, and I couldn't say anything. I watch her, letting the weight of her confession settle over me.

"It's not that I don't want to have a teahouse," she continues, her voice breaking slightly. "I do. It's my dream. But it doesn't have to be here. Maybe it shouldn't be here. These walls—they're my history, my roots, but they're also my cage. I think . . . I think I need to let them go to really grow."

Suddenly, I understand.

I remember the flood at Aspen Farms, how I'd fought so hard to rebuild, not because it was the right thing to do, but because I couldn't bear to let go of what I thought defined me. But holding on so tightly, I'd lost sight of what I truly needed.

"I get it," I say finally, my voice quiet. She looks up, her eyes fill with something between relief and surprise.

"You do?"

"Yeah," I say, nodding slowly. "I do."

For the first time, I see the dream she's been holding onto, tucked away behind the pain. It's not about leaving behind her passion but finding a way to honor it without being trapped by the past. And for some reason, knowing that makes me even more determined to help her.

Not just with the festival but with whatever comes next.

Chapter Thirteen

OPHELIA

The sound of my phone vibrating next to me on the nightstand, its light cutting through the darkness of my room, wakes me up. I groan, fumbling for it, half-blind from sleep.

Who would be texting me this late? Mom, possibly. There was a text from Mom, but that was from last night. She had to cancel our lunch today, but no, that was an old text—this text was new.

I read the message:

> Hey muffin, sorry to text you so early, but we have a meeting to attend when you close the shop tonight. Want me to swing by and walk with you to the town hall? I am off today. Meetings call for all of us, including you little lady.

What meeting? I blink, trying to focus, cursing myself for not leaving my phone downstairs like usual. I glanced at the clock—3:45 AM. My brain was slow to catch up, struggling to make sense of what the hell he was talking about.

I typed back:

What meeting?

I lay there, staring at my phone, waiting for his response. It didn't take long before the screen lit up again.

Well, the town hall is holding a meeting tonight for all festival attendees. We have to go over plans.

FESTIVAL! I jolt fully awake, anxiety rushing through me as I remember the steps I'd made with Emmett. I had promised to participate in the festival, step out of my comfort zone, and show the town more of myself. Before I could spiral any further, another text from him came through.

We need to work on a nickname for me... maybe stud muffin?

A smile tugs at my lips despite the early hour. I can picture Emmett amused with himself. I steady my hand to text back. My hands are freezing from my fan.

It hasn't even been 48 hours since I told you my plans, and the commitments are already starting? Is it too late to back out?

I know that isn't an option, and I can imagine him rolling his eyes at my comment. I bite my lip, a giggle erupting moments later, followed by a sigh. I close my eyes, praying I can find sleep once more. Poe stirs beside me, annoyed by the light from my phone moments prior. I call his name softly, hoping he would return to snuggling against me. Instead, he jumps off the bed and pads away into the shadows.

Another sigh escapes me, knowing sleep is elusive now . . . my mind already buzzing with thoughts of the day ahead. When my alarm blares later that morning, I groan, feeling the familiar throb of a headache forming behind my eyes. Waking up and falling back asleep always did this to me.

Sitting up slowly, I rub my temples and squint at the light filtering through the curtains. I usually invite it, but right now, it's not kind to the throbbing in my head. I mutter a quick prayer, hoping Poe isn't getting into trouble, and smile.

I go through my usual morning routine, slipping into the comforting rhythm of opening the tea shop. The quiet buzz of early morning settles around me like a soft blanket. The kitchen is cool, and the sunlight is still pale as it filters through the windows, casting a warm glow on the wooden counters. The air is crisp as I set about preparing my cinnamon rolls.

I knead the dough with care, the motions soothing in their repetition. The scent already beginning to fill the air. It's a fragrance that reminded me of home, of comfort—of mornings spent in the warmth of the shop, the world outside still waking up. I carefully arrange the rolls on the baking sheet, ensuring they are perfectly spaced, each swirl promising a melt-in-your-mouth sweetness.

As the oven heats up, the smell of cinnamon and sugar intensifies, mingling with the comforting scent of freshly steeped tea that begins to fill the air. The clock ticks closer to opening time, and I work with a familiar sense of purpose, knowing that the early birds will be arriving soon. I want to offer them something special, something warm and inviting to start their day, and cinnamon rolls always have that effect.

I place the tray in the oven, glancing at the small clock on the wall above the counter. The bell above the door chimes, a soft, tinkling sound that always makes me smile. I wipe my hands on my apron, straighten my hair, and turn to greet the first of my customers as they enter. I settle into my tasks effortlessly, making tea, pulling out jars of honey, and easily taking orders.

The early morning rush is always a bit of a dance—quick but pleasant. Something about the bustle of the shop, the clink of cups, the soft murmur of conversations makes me feel alive in a way I can't describe. But today is different. I notice something within me that I haven't felt in a long while—an eagerness to connect, to really listen.

When the last of the morning rush subsides and the shop is quiet, I lean back against the counter, a cup of chamomile tea cradled in my hands. I take a deep breath, allowing the moment's peace to settle over me. The cinnamon rolls now golden brown, their warm scent filling the shop, and for the first time in a while, I feel grounded and connected to this place—to the people who walk through the door and to the simple, everyday acts that brought me peace.

It was a reminder. That sometimes the smallest moments —like listening to a friend or offering a quiet smile—are the ones that make the day truly meaningful.

It wasn't until late afternoon, just after closing, that I hear a dog barking outside. Curious, I peek through the window and see Emmett walking up my driveway, a beagle trotting alongside him on a forest-green leash.

My heart does an unexpected flip.

He looks . . . really good.

A red flannel shirt stretches over his broad shoulders, and his black jeans fit him just right. I blush, spinning around and pretending to be busy, hoping he didn't catch me staring.

The door opens with a creak, and his voice fills the shop. "Knock, knock! Can I bring Gunner in?"

I play along, calling from the kitchen, "I presume Gunner isn't a human?"

Gunner barks in response, his wagging tail visible from where I stand. Just then, Poe darts from the kitchen, heading straight for the dog.

Emmett let out a panicked yelp. "Shit! I'm so sorry! I didn't even think of that!"

Heart racing, I rush out to stop whatever disaster might be about to unfold. I half-expected Poe to attack Gunner or, worse, Gunner to chase Poe around the shop. But to my surprise, Poe inches closer to the dog, sniffing him cautiously.

Gunner whines, rolling onto his back, clearly surrendering. Poe, as usual, remains unimpressed. He gives the dog a cursory sniff before sitting beside him and loafing like nothing happened.

Emmett and I exchange a glance.

"Huh . . ." I mumble, still in a bit of disbelief. "Let's keep an eye on them, but yes . . . Gunner is welcome to be inside."

Emmett nods, his gaze lingering on me longer than usual.

"I just need to close up and get dressed for the evening," I add, feeling my cheeks flush under his watchful eyes. "If you want, you can wait down here. I won't be long," I say, trying to sound casual as I start to take my hair down from its messy bun.

I notice Emmett shifting slightly, his gaze flickering away from me as if trying not to stare. "That works, Mossgrove," he replies, his voice a little quieter.

I hurry upstairs, closing the door behind me with a soft click. My heart is still racing. I can feel the heat in my cheeks as I rush to get ready. Why does he always make me feel this way? Shaking my head, I take a deep breath, focusing on the task. The town hall meeting approaches, and I have to prepare myself for whatever questions and stares await.

Once I'm ready, we drop off Gunner at Emmett's house before heading toward the main street. The evening air is cool as we walk side by side down Havenwood's cobblestone streets. The closer we get to the town hall, the more my anxiety starts to rear its head.

I pull my shawl tighter around me, trying to shield myself from the unease growing in my chest.

"You okay?" Emmett's voice is soft, his eyes searching my face as we walk.

"I'm fine," I lie, my voice more tense than intended. I wasn't fine.

The idea of walking into a crowded town hall with all those eyes on me made my heart race faster. My breaths come quick, and my chest feels tight as if my ribs are pressing on my lungs. Why now? I have been doing so good . . .

Tears threaten my eyes. As we near the large wooden doors of the town hall building, my feet become heavier with each step. The familiar pang of panic settling in, my mind spiraling with thoughts of how this meeting could go wrong.

As we step inside, the noise hits me—a wave of voices and people talking in groups, but everything shifts the second they see me. The noise quiets and every gaze lands on me. I freeze, my breath catching in my throat. My fingers instinctively clutch the edges of my shawl as if it can protect me from sudden attention.

"There she is!" someone calls out, and before I know it, people crowd around me, their voices merging into a blur of questions.

"Ophelia, what are you doing for your menu?"

"Are you doing tea pairings?"

"Will you cater the mayor's speech?"

The questions come too fast, one after the other, and I can't keep up. My head spins, and the walls of the room are closing in. My chest tightens even more, and my breaths become shallow.

I need to get out. I need space. Anything to stop the panic building inside me.

I feel Emmett's hand on my arm, grounding me for a moment. His voice is calm as he speaks to the crowd, managing the questions with ease, but I can hardly hear him over the sound of my heartbeat thundering in my ears. I squeeze my eyes shut, silently pleading for the anxiety to pass, for the ground to stop spinning beneath me.

Please, please, let me get through this.

Chapter Fourteen

EMMETT

I peer down at Ophelia. Her face is stark against the warm glow of the room. I feel a pang in my chest. Her hand grips tightly around her necklace, her knuckles white. I know she's spiraling.

Without thinking, I wrap my arms around her and pull her into a hug, hoping to shield her from the prying eyes and endless questions.

She smells like heaven, vanilla, and cinnamon. She melts against me, her body surrendering to the comfort of my embrace. However, this isn't enough to ease the panic still flashing in her eyes.

"Ophelia," I say softly, but she does not seem to hear me. Her breathing becomes more shallow, quick, and ragged. She's on the verge of a panic attack. I need to pull her back before she gets completely lost in it.

"Let's take this slow, everyone," I call out, my voice steady but firm. I need to create distance between her and the towns-people crowding around us. The questions are still coming. They aren't thinking, just curious—too curious for their own good.

And I can see it—Ophelia retreating, her mind folding inward, losing touch with reality.

"Ophelia," I say again, softer this time, leaning down so she could hear me and feel me closer. "Hey, hey, look at me. Breathe with me, okay?" I take her hand, gently placing it against my chest. "In and out, Ophelia. You're okay. Just breathe with me." I guide her through slow, deep breaths, exaggerating my movements so she could follow along.

It's shaky at first, her chest heaving as she struggles to find a rhythm, but I stay with her, murmuring quiet reassurances. I don't leave her side until I see the frantic look in her eyes soften, her breaths evening out.

Good . . . good.

At that moment, I realize she isn't just a stubborn home-body. She genuinely struggles. Something suffocating her ability to do things. Gradually, the world around us fades into the background. The noise, the people—it's just us now, and all that matters is helping her find her center again.

When her body finally relaxes, I brush her hair away from her face, my thumb gently caressing her cheek. "It's okay," I whisper. "You're okay."

Her hazel eyes look back at me.

Shit. Am I falling for Ophelia Mossgrove? This soon? This easy?

Out of the corner of my eye, I see movement, familiar —Dad.

His wide grin is plastered on his face, and he is staring at me and Ophelia.

"You leave that wonderful woman alone, you crazy people!" He shouts playfully, his voice booming through the room.

The crowd laughs, and I can feel the tension in the air ease. They apologize and offer Ophelia their well wishes before slowly filtering into the main room to settle down for the meeting.

Finally, her fingers lace between mine, and for a moment,

nothing else in this world matters. The warmth of her hand in mine makes everything feel more grounded, more real. It's like the world has shrunk to just the two of us.

My Dad's voice breaks through the daze. "How does that sound, Emmett?" he asks, looking directly at me. "Emmett?" he says again.

"Huh?" I stammer, embarrassed for zoning out in front of him. I tuck our hands out of sight, trying to cover up the moment.

He doesn't miss the small exchange, his eyes flicking between us for a beat too long before he clears his throat and gestures toward a large poster board.

"I said this—" He motions to the layout map, his voice a little more clipped now. "—will be the layout for the festival this year. Since we had to improvise on short notice last year, we're sticking to that plan and adding some space at the front of the town center. Thoughts?"

There is a flush creeping up my neck, a mix of frustration and embarrassment. I'd never been good at hiding my feelings, especially when my dad noticed something—anything—about me. But I brush it off, focusing on the map and trying to keep my mind in the present.

"Yeah, sounds good," I mutter, barely looking up from the board. His gaze lingers longer before he nods, satisfied enough with my response. I can't help but feel his eyes still on me, as if he is trying to read more into the situation than I am willing to show.

I nod, still not fully engaged in the conversation, though I pretend I am.

Ophelia hasn't let go of my hand.

I bend into her view, my voice low. "I need my hand back, Muffin. You can sit up here with me if it'll make you more comfortable, but I have to take over this rodeo now." I wink.

She blushes, her cheeks warming up with a color that makes me smile.

To my surprise, she nods before following me to the front of the room. She sits at the computer desk while I stand in front of the meeting table. The thought of everyone watching her from this angle crosses my mind, but she seems more at ease now, more grounded.

I begin to speak, ensuring I can still catch her eyes if she needs reassurance. "As you all know, my dad—the town's mayor and general glue—has had some health issues." I glance at him, and sure enough, there is that emotional look I expect. "So, from here on out, I will manage the festival. If you need to contact me with questions or concerns, you can send them to the town email. If you have my number, feel free to call as well."

I lay a stack of papers on the table containing the vendor schematic and my contact information. "Why don't we break into smaller groups to talk about the booths and some of the ideas we may have?" I glance at my dad again, who nods in agreement.

The room begins to break into clusters, with people huddling to discuss their plans.

I stay close to Ophelia as a few people tentatively approach. They are still unsure how to talk to her, but I won't let them skirt around her.

"What are your guys' plans for your sections this year?" I ask, smoothly bringing Ophelia into the conversation. "Ophelia's got some great ideas. Maybe she can share a few?"

Her eyes widen, her cheeks flushing. For a moment, I thought I'm pushing her too far, but then she clears her throat, and words begin to form, softly but surely explaining her plans.

"I actually have a few seasonal blends in mind," she says quietly but steadily. "I was thinking of offering some to-go options at the booth, along with new sourdough treats . . . and maybe some . . . muffins." Her eyes meet mine.

I shift in my seat. Everything she just said was gold, especially the muffins.

Mmm, muffins. Smiling the cheesiest smile I can muster, I squeeze her hand three times. She does it back.

The Tattered Basket manager across the table smiles warmly at Ophelia. "I would love to hear more about those blends. You always have such interesting combinations."

And just like that, the conversation picks up. People ask her questions about the teas and the baked goods. I watch as Ophelia's posture relaxes, her shoulders loosen, and even a tiny smile tugs at her lips. She's engaged, offering ideas and laughing along with the others.

And *God*, is she beautiful. The transformation is subtle, but it's happening, and I couldn't be more proud.

I look at her when the discussions wrap up and people start packing up to leave.

Really look at her. She's done it—she's stepped into the world she's always been so afraid of. She had a rough beginning but managed through, not giving up and not running. She was finding her voice, and for the first time, I realized she didn't need me to speak for her anymore—at least for today.

She found her rhythm, and the town wasn't just watching her now—they were listening.

"You did great," I say as we walk into the cool evening air, nudging her lightly.

"You made it easier," she replies softly.

"You did the hard part," I say, but as we walk side by side, I can't shake the feeling that things are changing. For both of us.

Chapter Fifteen

OPHELIA

I hadn't expected a crowd outside my home this early—not the morning after the town hall meeting. Yet, as I peer out the front window, I see familiar faces gathering in small clusters, chatting and glancing toward my door.

Was there another event I'd forgotten about?

Poe brushes against my leg before disappearing under my skirt and darting up the stairs, his little feet a rhythmic patter on the wooden steps. Morgan spots me through the glass and gave an enthusiastic wave. She is chatting with the same energy she'd had last night at the meeting.

Behind her stood Emmett, hands in his pockets, grinning as Florence says something that makes his shoulders shake with laughter. His ease irritates me more than it should.

Clearly, I woke up in a mood. I open the door with a deep breath and am greeted by the cool, damp scent of morning leaves. A ripple of light applause greets me, and I blink in surprise.

This is new.

"Well, good morning, Ophelia!" The manager of *The Tattered Basket* steps forward, beaming. "We couldn't let you open today without stopping by to tell you how wonderful last night was."

"Wonderful?" I echo, glancing around at the crowd. "That's . . . unexpected." I should have kept that to myself.

"Can we come in, or are you planning to keep us all out here, little lady?" Emmett's smooth and teasing voice cuts through the morning air. His gaze dips to my boots, a knowing glint in his eyes.

Before he can comment, I kick his boot lightly, earning a rich laugh.

"Fine, come in!" I say, stepping aside to let them in, my skirt brushing my legs as I move. The shop fills quickly, the air warming with the buzz of conversation. As I arrange chairs and pull teacups from their shelves, I feel the familiar rhythm of hosting settle into my bones. But something is different this time.

Morgan catches my arm as I pour her a cup of chamomile. "You've always had a gift, Ophelia. I don't think you realize how much this town appreciates you and what you bring to Havenwood."

Her words land heavier than I expect, and I scan the room. These aren't just customers or neighbors—they are people who care and see me. I love this—the hum of laughter, the warmth of connection—but the walls of my childhood home feel like they are closing in, too full of memories that stifle my breath.

Emmett must have caught my hesitation because he follows me into the kitchen and leans casually against the counter. "Need some help, Muffin?"

"Don't touch those!" I swat his hand away as he reaches for the teacups on my personal shelf.

"Noted," he says, holding up his hands in surrender, his lips quirk up in a maddening grin.

"Grab the ones from the hutch instead," I say, pointing.

He obliges, and we work side by side in companionable silence for a few minutes.

"So," he says after a while, "What's next for Havenwood's unofficial mayor of tea?"

I roll my eyes. "Unofficial mayor? Really?"

"Hey, I'm just saying," he teases. "You've got ideas, a crowd of admirers, and the boots for the job."

I open my mouth to argue but close it with a smile instead. "Brittany mentioned seasonal tea tastings," I say, testing the waters. "And others brought up hosting workshops or private events here."

"See?" He bumps my shoulder lightly. "You're already thinking big."

I hesitate, the words catching in my throat before I force them out. "I love all of this, Emmett. But . . . not here. Not in this house."

He froze, the teasing light in his eyes dimming as he set down the teacup he was holding. I face him fully. He doesn't say anything at first, his gaze steady on mine. Then, quietly, he says, "I know, Ophelia, I understand." He looks away and runs a hand through his hair, his expression softening. "I used to think Aspen Farms was everything. My one big dream. But after the flood . . ." He trails off, his jaw tightening. "Sometimes, you can't fix what's broken. Sometimes, you have to start fresh."

His words wrap around me like a balm, soothing the ache I hadn't known how to name.

"But you're not running, Ophelia," he says firmly. "We're not running. We'll figure this out together."

"Together?" I whisper.

He smiles, and something about how he says it makes my heart stutter. What did "together" mean? How was he going to help me rebuild my dream? I'm not sure, but for the first time in a long time, I'm not afraid to find out.

Chapter Sixteen

EMMETT

The creaky front door closing behind me echoes through the small hallway, signaling the end of the morning's unexpected hustle.

I stand there momentarily, taking it all in, letting the silence settle around me. The air outside is crisp, but the warmth inside Ophelia's teahouse is a comfort—one that still feels foreign despite my growing familiarity with it.

Together.

The word hung in my mind, curling in like the steam from the cups I'd carried to tables, hanging heavy in the air like the smell of chamomile and muffins that seem to linger in the walls of the place. She hadn't said it, but I could feel it—the relief in her eyes, the tiny cracks that had started to form in the walls she'd built around herself.

She'd let me help, even if only for a morning, and that meant something.

I press my back against the doorframe, my hands in my pockets, staring out at the town as it bustles around in its quiet routine. I hear the faint hum of conversations from the teahouse, still alive with energy even though the crowd has dissipated. More than I'd expected, a lot had changed in that room in just a few hours. More than I'd hoped for, maybe.

Ophelia was struggling with the idea of letting go—of letting her teahouse go and of letting herself go. I could see it every time she hesitated. Every time she fought the pull of the people who wanted to help her, every time she looked at the teahouse with a certain sadness in her eyes as if it were the only thing holding her together.

She didn't know what to do with the space, with herself, with what awaited her on the other side of those doors. But today?

Today, she'd opened up in a way I hadn't seen before. She hadn't just opened the door to the teahouse for the people who cared about her—she'd opened herself up, just a crack, and let a little bit of the light in.

I am not naive enough to think it's fixed. It isn't. But I had done something—I had shown her that she wasn't alone. That there was no shame in needing others. That there was room in this world, in her life, for more than just her quiet teashop.

Together.

It was a simple promise. One I wasn't even sure she'd understood at the time. But I did. I knew exactly what I meant. I wasn't just talking about the teahouse. I was talking about everything—the burden she'd been carrying on her own, the fear of change that seemed to trap her in place, the ache that only someone who truly understood her could see.

I am not going anywhere.

My phone buzzes in my pocket, pulling me out of my thoughts. A message from Dad. He'd checked in after the morning, knowing I'd probably be busy with Ophelia's teahouse business:

How's Ophelia? Everything okay?

I sigh, a smile pulling at the corners of my mouth. Dad is

always worried. But I can't blame him. He'd watched Ophelia struggle with this town for years, and now he saw her finally begin to figure it out.

All good.

I hit send and shove my phone back in my pocket. It is not the whole truth. But it's enough for now. The real work was beginning, and I wasn't sure if Ophelia knew it yet. I wasn't about to leave her hanging, though. I shove my hands in my coat pockets. This next part was going to be hard.

There was still the matter of the teahouse and what to do with it. Something Ophelia needed to be laid out for her, and well . . . I had no problem getting that started. I'd made up my mind—I would help her sell it, but not before showing her there was another way, another future for her.

A future outside the walls of her childhood home.

A future that didn't have to be defined by the teahouse or the quiet routine she clung to. She had so much more to offer, and if I could just make her see that.

But once again, I wasn't in the business of hurting people who didn't deserve it. No matter how badly I wanted to take charge, make things happen, and be the hero in this story.

I knew I couldn't do it without her blessing. It was about respecting her, her life, and her choices.

I push open the door, stepping inside to find Ophelia behind the counter, tightening the lid on a tea jar. She looks up at me, her gaze soft but guarded. I want to keep this simple. There's already so much unspoken between us, so many words that have hung in the air like an unplayed song.

Her eyes are still damp, but she smiles anyway. "Forgot cookies or something?" she asks, her voice gentle as if trying to make light of the tension.

I hesitate, then blurt it out, my words coming out shakier than I expected but still carrying the weight of everything I've been thinking. "Let me go to the realtor's office. Let me help you get this started. I want to help you, Ophelia, but I need your permission."

The room feels still for a moment, the air thick with everything that hasn't been said. She fidgets with the jar in her hands, her fingers running over the label before she looks up at me again.

Her eyes glisten. "Yes," she whispers, her voice barely audible. There's no hesitation. My heart beats louder than any rational thought.

Before I realize it, I'm out the door, the weight of her words anchoring me, and one place is in my mind now.

The realtor's office is just around the corner, tucked between a couple of the local shops. The bell above the door jingles as I walk in, the familiar scent of wood and ink greeting me.

"Emmett Sterling!" The receptionist calls with a smile. "What can I do for you today?"

"I need to speak with an agent about the teahouse at the edge of town for . . . selling reasons," I say, giving her a half-smile as I flop into a seat.

She looks stunned.

But I divert. "How is everything?"

"Busy! The town's been growing, and more people are looking to buy than we anticipated."

I nod, trying to focus. I am not here for small talk. I'm here to see if we can make some progress on getting answers regarding Ophelia's place. *If* we can even sell it. The thought still feels strange, as if it doesn't quite fit into the puzzle of my plans.

The agent, a middle-aged man with gray hair and a

professional air, calls me back. We shake hands as I follow him to his office, sitting across from his desk as he flips through a few papers.

"So, Emmett," he begins, "I understand you're looking to list a property on the edge of town. A local teahouse, correct?"

I nod. The thought already weighing on my chest. "Yes. Ophelia's Teahouse. She's. . . she's not sure what to do with it anymore. It's too much for her to handle alone. She's been thinking about selling it for a while, but—" I pause, wondering how much to say. "She's been struggling to make the decision."

The agent scribbles something down on his pad, looking at me thoughtfully. "I can imagine. It's a tough market, though, especially for commercial properties. And that place, while charming, isn't exactly in the most ideal location for high traffic, and well . . . it isn't exactly up to standards. It is an old home with newer renovations, but the odds we'd find a buyer wanting the home as is?" His tongue clicked a few times.

I swallow. "What do you mean?"

He peers up from his notes, his expression serious. "It's just—well, it's on the edge of town. It's tucked away, and while people love it, it's not drawing in the foot traffic that a place like that needs to stay viable. Not without a major overhaul."

A knot forms in my stomach. "So, what are we looking at? What can we do?"

He leans back in his chair, clearly choosing his words carefully. "We could list it, sure. But the market right now is not favorable. If we're looking at a quick sale, we'd have to drop the price significantly, and even then, it could take months."

I let the words settle in my mind. Months? She didn't have months. She needed something to shift—now. I stand, my mind racing. "Okay, thanks for the insight. Let's keep this in mind and maybe meet again soon." *Shit.*

The agent nods, looking at me curiously. "No problem. We'll be in touch."

A sense of frustration pours over me as I walk out of the office and into the cold air. The meeting didn't go the way I'd hoped it would go. *Shit, shit, shit.*

I stroll, my thoughts circling. I have to make this work for both of us.

I rest against the cool brick wall, staring at my phone screen as I dial James's number. My thoughts are a tangled mess—too many worries and things I can't control. I need to talk to someone, and James was always the one who could talk me down and put things into perspective. It rang twice before he picked up, his voice as familiar and steady as it always was.

"Emmett, buddy, what's up little shit?"

I sigh, trying to gather my thoughts. "I don't know, man," I say, feeling the weight of it all in my chest. "I thought I had a plan. I thought I could help Ophelia. Get the teahouse sold, get her out of there, get her a fresh start. But the realtor . . . he says it's gonna be a tough sell, man. And it's not just that. The place is on the edge of town. Sure, it's got its charm, but it's not exactly what people want. I don't know if she'll get what it's worth."

There's a pause on the other end. I can almost hear him thinking, processing everything I just threw at him.

"Easy to want to fix everything right away, right?" he says calmly. "We're guys. We like solutions. But listen, Emmett, you need to give it some time. You're trying to control everything, and that's not how this is gonna work. This isn't just about selling a building. There's more going on here. And maybe you don't have to fix it all right now. Things need to fall into place, but you've gotta give them the space to do that."

My shoulders slump. He's not wrong. I'd been so focused on solving Ophelia's problems that I hadn't really stopped to think about what was actually going on. Not just with her, but with me. Maybe I wasn't in the right headspace either.

"You're telling me to just . . . wait?" I ask, running a hand through my hair.

"Not exactly, wait," he says with a chuckle. "More like, let things breathe. Give it time. You're doing the right thing, being there for her, but don't rush to fix everything. Sometimes, things have to break apart before they can come back together. It might not be clear right now, but you're not supposed to have all the answers, Emmett. You never do. You just need to show up."

I close my eyes briefly, my head back against the wall. I had to admit, he makes sense. I am too focused on trying to force a solution, trying to push her into something before she's ready. The pressure to have it all figured out is suffocating.

"Yeah," I mutter, more to myself than to him. "I've been trying to do too much. I thought everything would fall into place if I just got the teahouse sold. But it's not that simple, is it?"

"Nope," James says. "It's not. And that's okay. Look, I've got a feeling there's more going on here, something bigger than just the teahouse. You're doing the right thing. Just keep doing what you're doing, being there for her, and trust that the pieces will fall into place when they're supposed to."

Of course, he knew there was something bigger going on. I hadn't stopped unloading my problems onto him since we were kids. James knew everything—every detail, every twist and turn that made me who I am, and what made me Emmett Sterling. I hated that he could see me so clearly, but at the same time, I couldn't deny how grateful I was. He was the only one who truly understood, even when I couldn't stand it.

I let his words sink in, a quiet relief washing over me. I didn't have to fix everything. I just had to be there. The rest would figure itself out.

"I'll tell you what. I might have a few answers for you, but you've gotta give it a little time. Don't rush it. I'll be in touch soon."

I raise an eyebrow, confused. "What kind of answers?"

"Don't worry about it for now, little shit." He says with a grin I can practically hear. "Just trust me. You'll know when the time's right. Just take it easy for a bit."

I laugh. "Alright. I'll take your word for it. I guess I'll just sit tight and see what happens."

"Good man. Take care, bud. I'll check in soon." The call ends, and I stand there momentarily, staring out at the quiet street. I don't have all the answers. I don't even know what the next step is.

But James was right about one thing—I don't have to solve everything today. I just have to show up. And maybe that was enough for now. I take a deep breath, letting the weight on my chest lift just a little. Things were complicated, sure. But I was in it. For better or worse, I was in it.

And somehow, that feels like a step in the right direction.

Chapter Seventeen

OPHELIA

I stir the dried blueberries into the mix, careful not to crush them. Their tiny bursts of flavor fill the air with a gentle sweetness. The scent of cinnamon follows, mingling with the softness of vanilla and the warmth of baked oats.

It's the beginning of something new—a blend I'd never quite tried—my version of a blueberry muffin in a teacup. I start with the basics: black tea, the backbone of many of my blends. I want something robust that can carry the layers of flavor without getting lost in them. Then, I add the dried blueberries, plump but firm, their color a reminder of summer mornings.

Then it's cinnamon, a touch of nutmeg, and a sprinkle of sugar crystals to mimic that buttery muffin finish. The more I mix, the more the smell seems to wrap around me, pulling me deeper into the process. I add a hint of vanilla bean for that rich, comforting note that always makes things feel like home.

There was something almost meditative about curating a blend, about combining ingredients until they were more than just their individual parts. Each ingredient was like a memory, a story, a piece of something I could touch, feel, and share with someone else through their senses.

I stir slowly, feeling the edges of the blend come together, the colors deepening as the dried herbs and fruits swirl together. I let the mixture sit for a moment, inhaling the scent that now seems to cling to the air. It's perfect—rich and familiar yet new—just how I want it to be.

With a quiet smile, I grab my notebook, its pages worn from years of tea blending, and scribble down.

Name: ???

That feels right. I can name it later.

For now, I want to bask in the perfection of what I've created. The teapot clinks as I set it down on the counter, steam swirling up, a reminder of the room's warmth. I take a deep breath, feeling the quiet calm of the moment wrap around me like a blanket. There is a fleeting peace here, in the silence, the blend that is now part of me, and the rhythmic motions so familiar.

I close my eyes, letting myself enjoy the stillness. That's when I hear it. The scrape of boots against the wood floors. A quiet pause at the threshold. A deep breath.

And then, Emmett's voice. "You've been busy."

I open my eyes, startled out of my thoughts, and there he stood. Perching against the doorframe, crossing his arms, his presence as undeniable as the breeze that ruffles the leaves outside. He's watching me, a half-smile tugging at the corner of his lips. "Of course, I've been busy," I say, forcing a casualness I don't feel, wiping my hands on the apron around my waist. "It's a tea shop, Emmett. What else would I be doing?"

He pushes off from the door, stepping into the room's warmth. "I'm guessing you're not just mixing tea blends for fun." He examines the scattered ingredients and the notebook I forgot to close. His eyes linger on the page. "What's the name?"

I sigh, tapping the notebook with my finger. "Not sure."

"Keeping it a mystery, huh?"

I smile softly. "For now."

He chuckles but doesn't say anything else, his gaze shifting to the small wooden table where I set the blend. "Well, I've got news."

I straighten, sensing the shift in his tone, the weight of something pressing against him that isn't just curiosity. "News? What kind of news?"

He pauses, stepping closer, the air between us growing heavier. I'm sure if I like the look in his eyes—it's hard to read. Something hidden beneath the surface of my skin bubbles up. It happens whenever he is near.

"I met with the agent today," he says, the words coming out carefully. "I don't know if you're going to like what he had to say, but the place . . . it's not as easy a sell as I thought."

My heart sinks. The world seems to tilt for a moment. My hands freeze, gripping the table's edge for stability. The weight of his words hits me harder than I expect. I should have seen this coming, but I hadn't—not really. I hadn't let myself think about the practical side of all this. The idea of letting go, of selling this house, of starting over—it was terrifying.

"The place is beautiful, but it's not in the best location," Emmett continues, his voice lowering. "And the price . . . well, I think the realtor's right. It might be hard to get what you're asking for. I just wanted you to know."

I take a deep breath, forcing myself to meet his gaze. I had been preparing for this, hadn't I?

In my gut, I'd always known that this was a mountain I'd have to climb. It wouldn't be easy. It was never going to be easy.

I can feel the familiar weight of my fears and doubts pressing in. I built this life, this identity, around this place. And now, it felt like I was losing my grip.

But then, something shifts inside me, quiet but resolute. I

had been through worse. I had lost things, even people, and I had become stronger and more confident of who I was. If I survived that, I could survive this.

"Okay," I say, my voice steady despite the tightness in my chest. "Another mountain to climb. It's fine. I can do this."

Emmett's eyes soften, but there is something deeper in his gaze than concern or sympathy. He reaches for me, his hand gently cupping my face. The touch is electric and tender, as if grounding me at that moment.

"Ophelia," he whispers, his voice low. "You don't have to do this alone."

Before I can respond and find the words to explain how much that meant, he leans in, his lips about to brush against mine.

It's a soft movement, tentative, like a question. The moment hangs there, suspended between us as if the world forgot to keep turning. My heart pounds in my chest, my breath catching in my throat. I am frozen in place, unable to move or breathe, just lost in the feel of him so close.

But just as quickly as it came, he pulls back, a playful grin on his lips. "Guess I got ahead of myself." His voice light and teasing. "Sorry, little lady."

I stand there, completely still, as he steps away, his words echoing in my mind. I can't move. I can't think. My body frozen in the wake of what had just happened. I watch him leave the room, my mind racing, my pulse still thudding in my ears. My lips still tingle where his had been, and I knew one thing for sure: tonight, alone in the silence—I would be thinking about this moment.

Dammit, Emmett Sterling. Next time, just kiss me.

Chapter Eighteen

EMMETT

I shift in bed, trying to find a comfortable position, but the throbbing pulse in my chest and the tightness in my pants won't let me. I close my eyes, replaying the moment—her face so close to mine, her breath almost mingling with mine.

I nearly kissed her. I *almost* kissed her.

The thought makes me tense up, my body reacting in ways I don't want to deal with right now. My heart's still hammering like it's trying to break free from my ribs.

That close. God. It was all there: the tension, the heat, how she looked at me like she wanted me to do it. I groan and shift again, throwing the blanket off.

The cool air hits my skin, but it doesn't help. I'm frustrated, to say the least. Frustrated with myself for hesitating, frustrated with how I can't get her out of my head, even now. Her smile, the way she looked at me like she didn't know whether to run or lean in, the way her lips parted just before I pulled away.

It's only been one night, but it feels like days. My phone buzzes from the nightstand, breaking through the fog of my thoughts. I reach for it, still not fully awake, my fingers brushing the screen to see the message.

It's a picture of Ophelia, her green Tony Lamas boots front and center. She's leaning against the counter in the teahouse, the familiar, cozy space behind her, a smirk tugging at her lips. The caption reads:

Best boots ever (kiss my ass, Emmett).

I stare at the photo . . .

Seeing her, even in something as simple as a pair of boots, hits me harder than I expect. Those boots . . . the way they fit her, the way she carries herself when she wears them—it's all sexy as hell . . . even if that color was awful.

I bite back a smile, the humor in her message striking a chord with me. But beneath the teasing words, there's something else—a spark.

A challenge. And that's the part that does something to me.

I feel a sharp jolt of desire, and my pulse kicks up again, a little faster this time. I reread the caption.

"I gladly would, little lady." I rub a hand over my face, groaning in frustration again, feeling a throb of heat settle low in my stomach. What the hell is it about her? Every time I think I've got a handle on this . . . this—whatever it is between us—she goes and does something like this. Something that sets me off all over again.

Slow down. You were the one that made the move.

I swipe the screen away and toss my phone aside, trying to will myself to relax. But it's no use. Her image, the teasing, the challenge in her words—it's all too much.

I can't stop imagining her standing in front of me, the way her smile softens when she lets down her guard.

Hell, I want her. It's not just the teasing or the way she challenges me. There's something deeper there, something I don't quite understand yet, but I can't deny it. And it's driving me crazy.

I take a deep breath, reaching for my jeans, trying to get dressed without thinking about her too much, but I can't stop. I decide to take a shower. Anything to make this throbbing stop. Anything to release the way this woman made me feel.

I need Ophelia Dawn Mossgrove—in more ways than one.

The day is dragging on like molasses.

After my boyish fit this morning, I down a few cups of black coffee to prepare for the hundreds of packages waiting. Dad called to let me know they needed me. The pressure's mounting, everything happening all at once, the steady stream of deliveries, the constant rush of people and packages. The weight is crushing me, but the extra hours and overtime will pay off.

I keep telling myself that as I haul one more box into the back of my truck and set off down the familiar route. *At least they called you in for work.*

As I drive, the sun's starting to dip lower in the sky, casting a golden glow over the sleepy town. Havenwood's the kind of place that looks even better at twilight—quiet streets, the soft sound of birds in the trees. I wish I could relax and take in the scenery, but I'm already thinking about the bed waiting for me and how my muscles ache from the long hours.

One more stop. One more delivery.

I turn the corner onto my driveway, the small, worn-out house coming into view. I'm ready for some quiet. Some peace.

I park my truck at the curb, the engine clicking as it cools. As I step out, my body feels like Jell-O, and the tension in my shoulders is so thick it's almost painful.

The mailbox is still half-full, but I ignore it, walking up the cracked stone path toward the front door. That's when I see her—Ophelia.

She's standing there, just past the porch, her hands tucked into the pockets of her cardigan, her hair slightly messy, like she's been out in the wind. She looks like she doesn't belong in this moment, in this setting, yet somehow, she does.

As usual, she's effortlessly perfect, even in the most unassuming way. She doesn't even notice me at first. Her eyes are focused on the flowers by the porch starting to wilt. I can feel my heartbeat in my throat as I take a step closer, her presence hitting me like a wave, sudden and overwhelming.

"Ophelia?" I manage to say, my voice hoarse from exhaustion. Her head snaps up, and she smiles, a warm, genuine smile that tightens my chest.

"Hey," she says, her voice soft and soothing—like music after a long day. I hope I'm not interrupting."

I blink, unsure if I'm dreaming. "It's fine, Mossgrove."

"Well . . . *Sterling*." She shrugs a little, a teasing light in her eyes. "I figured you could use a break."

I chuckle under my breath, wiping a hand across my face. "You could say that. What are you doing here?"

She steps closer, and for a moment, I swear she will reach out and touch me, but she pulls back at the last second. It's almost like she's playing with me, keeping me on edge like always.

"I thought you could use some company," she says, glancing at my truck with the dirty cargo bed.

Uh-huh—*she's* lonely.

I let out a tired sigh. I can see the concern in her eyes, the subtle way she watches me like she's trying to figure something out. It's the same look she always gives me, like she's trying to peel back layers and get to the truth of things.

"Well," she says after a beat. "I figured I'd make it easier for you. I brought dinner."

My eyes widen, and for a moment, the exhaustion slips away. "Dinner?" I huff. *Thank you, God.* Thank you for this fine woman and whatever divine food she has brought.

She gives me a playful smile. "I thought I'd cook. I mean, I know how crazy it gets during the busy seasons. No one should have to fend for themselves on top of it all."

I can't help but grin, my heart suddenly lifting. "You brought dinner for me?"

"Yep," she replies, "I even brought some of those pumpkin chocolate cookies you like."

She is perfect.

My chest squeezes with something unfamiliar, a warmth that's hard to put into words. She remembers the little things I never thought anyone would notice.

"Okay, now I'm interested," I admit, taking a step closer, the exhaustion temporarily forgotten. "What kind of dinner?"

"Well," she says, "I've got roasted chicken, mashed potatoes, and the works. It's a little rustic, but I think it'll do the trick."

I take a deep breath, fighting the grin threatening to break across my face. "I'm sold, Little Lady. Get in the house." I playfully tap her back end and say teasingly. "Now."

Ophelia laughs, and that sound wraps around me and pulls me in like everything in the world could be okay if I just let go and let her in. "Well, I would, but the door is locked," she giggles.

I glance at her, my heart racing in a way it shouldn't. But it's Ophelia. Of course, it's racing. I can't stop myself from looking at her the way I do. I can't help it.

"Oh yeah," I say. I unlock the door, and Gunner runs toward us. She steps past me into the house, and I follow her inside, my mind still spinning from the unexpected visit and the surprising way she's become someone I don't want to let go of. I shut the door behind us.

Little Lady is in my house. *Hell yeah.*

Chapter Nineteen

OPHELIA

I am inside Emmett's house.

I just had *dinner*—at *Emmett's house.*

My heart pounds. He stretches out on the worn armchair, one leg lazily slung over the other, his mug balanced on his knee. His presence fills the space in a way that doesn't overwhelm—it just feels . . . right.

He's looking at the fire crackling in the hearth, but I can feel his attention flicker back to me like it always does. "I've got to ask," he starts, his tone playful, but his eyes are warm. "Do you still play with dolls using your feet?"

The question hangs in the air for a second, and then I burst out laughing. It's not a delicate laugh, either—it's loud and raw, making me bury my face in my hands out of sheer embarrassment.

"You did not just bring that up!" I peek through my fingers to see him grinning, completely unapologetic.

"Oh, I did," he says, leaning forward. "You were a sight, you know. Legs up in the air, one Barbie in each foot, making them talk to each other like that was the most normal thing in the world."

"I was eight!" I protest, though I'm laughing so hard that I can barely breathe. "And, for the record, it was a genius way to multitask."

"Sure, genius," he teases, his grin widening. "But don't think I didn't notice you doing it when you were ten."

I groan, shaking my head. "You've got a freakishly good memory."

"Comes in handy," he says, sipping his drink. "I always knew where you'd be. If you weren't singing to your mom's garden in the backyard, you were inside with those dolls, creating elaborate soap operas."

I feel my cheeks heat, but there's no sting to his words— just a soft warmth that wraps around me like a blanket. "You know, you weren't exactly subtle, always hanging around, watching me from the fence," I counter.

He smirks, unrepentant. "What can I say? You were the entertainment."

After that, we fall into an easy silence, the kind that doesn't need filling. The fire crackles, and I watch the way the light dances across the planes of his face. His features are softer now, and he's letting his guard down just enough to let me in.

"Do you remember that one summer?" I ask after a while, my voice quieter. "The one where my dad built that swing in the backyard?"

He nods, a small smile tugging at his lips. "Yeah. You used to twist it up as tight as it would go and let it spin you until you were dizzy."

"You used to push me," I remind him, leaning back in my chair. "Then run to the other side of the yard like I was some kind of slingshot."

He chuckles, the sound low and rich. "Your dad wasn't too happy about that. Kept yelling at me to quit it before I broke the swing."

We fall quiet again, and I sip my tea, feeling the weight of the memories settle between us. They're not heavy, though— they're light, like leaves drifting on the surface of a stream.

"Do you ever think about those days?" I ask softly, not looking at him. "All the time," he admits, his voice just as low. "They were good days, weren't they?"

I nod, my chest tightening. "They were."

Neither of us said much after that, but we don't need to. The silence stretches, but it's not empty—it's full of shared history, unspoken words, and a connection that feels as steady as the ground beneath us. Emmett leans forward to set his mug on the table, and for a moment, I think he might say something more, but he just sinks back into the chair, his eyes closing as if he's content to let the quiet carry us through.

I lean back, too, letting the warmth of the fire and his presence fill the spaces I hadn't realized were empty. Together, but silent. It's enough.

For now, it's enough.

The warm water laps at my shoulders as I sink deeper into the tub, the steam curling into the cool night air that seeps through the slightly cracked window. A hint of lavender and chamomile fills the bathroom, the oils mixing with the bathwater and wrapping around me like a hug.

The house is quiet, except for the occasional creak of the floorboards as it settles for the night. Dinner at Emmett's. The thought loops in my mind like a favorite melody—his easy laughter, the way he listened when I spoke about my day, and the simple comfort of sharing a meal in his home.

It wasn't extravagant or monumental, but it was . . . something.

Something I hadn't allowed myself to experience in so long—a connection, uncomplicated and warm.

I stretch my toes, letting them poke above the water, and

smile. My world is changing. It's not just about Emmett, though he seems to be the catalyst. It's everything. Letting Florence help me at the tea house, venturing into town more often, taking a moment to truly listen to the stories of the people I serve. I rest against the tub and close my eyes, my heartbeat filling the quiet.

Change isn't easy. It's messy and unpredictable, forcing you to confront parts of yourself you'd rather keep hidden. But tonight, as the warmth of the bath soothes my muscles, I feel a flicker of something I hadn't expected: pride. I'm doing it. I'm stepping out beyond the teacups, my routine, and the carefully constructed walls I've spent years building. I'm doing the hard thing.

The memory of Emmett's face flickers behind my closed eyelids—his teasing smirk when he mentioned the dolls, the softness in his voice when he reminisced about summers spent pushing me on the swing, the way his presence felt like a steady hand guiding me through all this change.

I sigh, a mixture of exhaustion and contentment washing over me. It feels good, this growing. Hard, but good. The water is cool by the time I climb out, wrapping myself in a thick towel. I pad to my room, the worn floorboards cold against my feet, and slip under the covers. The lavender from the bath lingers on my skin, and I breathe it in, letting it lull me toward sleep. As my eyes grow heavy, I think about the person I'm becoming—the version of myself who is brave enough to try, grow, and love. I let myself feel proud.

The last thing I remember before sleep takes me is the warmth of the memory, the echo of Emmett's laugh, and the quiet hum of possibility filling the air.

Chapter Twenty

OPHELIA

I sit on the edge of the worn armchair, legs crossed, hands neatly folded in my lap.

"Alright, Ophelia." Dr. Curler's voice comes through my phone's speaker, calm and steady, like the constant rhythm of a well-brewed pot of tea. "Let's talk about how you're feeling today. What's on your mind?"

I exhale slowly. I've gotten better at answering her questions without feeling like I'm letting the weight of my heart crush my chest. Sometimes, though, it's harder than others. Today feels like one of those days where the words don't come easily, where the feelings swirl together in a mess I can't quite sort out.

"Well," I begin, my voice tentative. "I guess I've been thinking about . . . Emmett—a lot."

Dr. Curler doesn't interrupt, doesn't rush me. She waits, and I'm grateful for it because sometimes, it takes me a minute to get the words out.

"I . . . I don't know. It's like everything has changed. I've never been someone who lets other people in, and now, it feels like I'm doing it without even realizing how much I'm opening up to him." I pause, chewing on my bottom lip as I try to gather the right words. "I don't know if I'm ready for all of this . . . but at the same time, it's like there's this pull, you know? I can't explain it. He just . . . he makes me want to try. He makes me feel like maybe there's more to life than the little world I've built around myself."

Dr. Curler's voice is soft but encouraging. "It sounds like you're really acknowledging your feelings for him. That's progress, Ophelia. You've been so cautious for so long, and now, here you are, letting yourself feel something new."

"I didn't want to," I admit, the weight of that truth settling over me like a thick blanket. "I didn't want to admit it. I didn't want to feel something for him because I didn't want to risk losing control of my life. I thought . . . I thought if I let someone in, everything would fall apart."

"And now?" she asks gently.

"Now . . . I don't know," I murmur, fiddling with the edge of my cardigan. "It's terrifying, but I'm learning that control isn't everything. It's just . . . it's so much easier to stay in my little bubble, where everything's safe and familiar. But I can't do that anymore. I can't pretend like I'm okay with being alone."

Dr. Curler pauses for a moment, allowing my words to sink in. I can almost hear her smile through the phone, how she always does when she's proud of me for realizing something important. "You've come so far, Ophelia. You've moved mountains. I know it might not feel like it, but you've really started to let go of the things holding you back."

Her words hit me in the chest, soft but firm, like a wave crashing over me. She's right in a way I hadn't realized until now. I've spent so much of my life building walls, thinking they were the only thing keeping me safe. And now, here I am, standing on the edge of something new, something uncertain —and I'm allowing it.

"I'm really proud of you," Dr. Curler continues. "You've been working hard, and it's clear that you're facing your fears head-on. This journey you're on, with Emmett, with yourself —it's not easy, but you're doing it. You're doing phenomenally well."

I can feel a lump forming in my throat. The validation and encouragement are exactly what I've needed but never asked for. It's like a lifeline, pulling me back from the edge of doubt that always tries to creep in.

"Thank you," I whisper, my voice thick with emotion. "I . . . I didn't think I could get here. I didn't think I could ever want to be with someone, to let myself feel worthy of more than just this little world I've built. Maybe I deserve to be happy."

Dr. Curler's voice is filled with warmth. "You absolutely deserve it, Ophelia. Remember that. You are worthy of love, of happiness, of everything you want. It's okay to let yourself have those things."

I close my eyes momentarily, letting her words burrow into my heart. I know they're true, even though it's hard for me to fully believe them. But I'm trying. I'm trying to trust myself more. "I'm going to take it slow, but I'm going to let myself feel everything. I'm going to let myself be open. Even if it scares me."

"That's a wonderful plan, Ophelia," Dr. Curler says, her voice full of pride. "You're doing so much better than you realize. I can't wait to hear about the next step you take."

I smile a little, feeling lighter than I have in a long time. "Thanks, Dr. Curler. I appreciate everything you've helped me with."

"Of course. It's my pleasure. Remember, you're always doing more than you think. You're not alone in this."

I inhale deeply, the weight on my chest easing for the first time in a long while. "Thank you. I'll talk to you next week."

After a moment's pause, she says, "Take care of yourself, Ophelia. And remember to be kind to yourself."

I hung up the call, and my phone felt a little less heavy in my hand. I recline back against the armchair, staring out the window, a soft smile tugging at my lips. I can do this.

The air is cool and crisp as I step outside, the smell of moss and damp earth filling my lungs. I go down the familiar, worn path behind the teahouse that leads to Mossgrove Creek.

The sound of the water trickling over the rocks is comforting, like an old friend whispering secrets I haven't heard in years. I've walked this path countless times in my life, but today it feels different. I find a spot along the creek near the large oak tree that's always stood tall beside the water. Its roots stretch like fingers, cradling the earth beneath me, and I sit on one of the low, wide branches.

The soft hum of the creek fills my ears, and I let my feet dangle just above the water, feeling the freezing cold air on my bare skin. The world feels quiet and still, and for a moment, it's as if I'm alone in this small pocket of peace, untouched by the world's worries. But the quiet is loud in its own way, isn't it?

I close my eyes and let the memories flood my mind—memories of when I was a little girl, my parents' laughter echoing in the distance, the joy of running through these woods pretending to be a wild animal or an explorer on some grand adventure. In the days when everything felt within reach, like the world was made of magic and wonder, I was free to dream as big as I wanted.

Tears well up in my eyes, unbidden, and I let them fall, one by one, down my cheeks. It's not sadness, exactly, but a release. A recognition of how much I've held on to, how much I've buried deep within me, all the pain of growing up and trying to hold things together. The ache of keeping my family's legacy in my hands, of taking on more than I was ever meant to. The feeling of being stuck.

I cry for all of it, for the parts of me that I've silenced, for the dreams I let slip through my fingers. But then, something shifts. The sobs fade, and I feel the cool breeze brush against my skin. A lightness fills my chest, and for the first time in what feels like forever, I stand up, pulling my feet from the creek's edge. I'm smiling through my tears now, not from sadness but something else—a sense of release.

A sense of rediscovery. Without thinking, I spin in a circle, my arms outstretched as I twirl around the creek. My feet sink into the earth, the dirt cool and firm beneath me, grounding me. The tears are dry now, but my heart feels lighter and freer. I laugh, a sound that feels like it's been trapped in me for years. I feel the weight of the world lifting, if only for a moment.

I don't care if anyone sees me. I don't care if it's ridiculous. I twirl again, my feet leaving the ground just a little bit as I dance by the water. I raise my voice, singing a song I haven't heard in years, but it flows from my lips like it's always been there, waiting to be set free. My voice rings out, full and strong, bouncing off the trees and the creek.

It feels so natural, like something I used to do all the time —before the world became so heavy, before the weight of responsibility pressed down on me. I feel the dirt on my feet, the roughness of the earth beneath me, and it's grounding. I feel more connected to myself than I have in ages.

I'm not just Ophelia, the teahouse owner. I'm Ophelia, the girl who once ran wild in these woods, free and full of life. I stop spinning, my heart racing with excitement, a smile wide on my face. The sun filters through the trees, casting dappled light on the ground, and for a moment, I simply stand there, breathing in the air, letting the world settle around me.

I'm still me. I've always been me. I just had to find my way back. I feel whole. I feel like I've found my center again, the part of me that's been missing all these years. I'm ready to share that with someone else.

I'm not sure what tomorrow holds, but today, I'm dancing in the dirt, singing to the creek, and finally feeling like myself again. *Live a lotta bit.*

Chapter Twenty-One

EMMETT

James leans against the bar, nursing a beer like it was the best thing he'd tasted in years. It's good to see him, really good. The guy had been like a big brother since we were kids, and even though life had taken us down different roads, the bond was still there—unshakable.

"You look like you've been running on fumes," James says, his mouth quirking into a smirk.

"Peak season. Guess they need me now," I reply, swaying my drink. "Mail doesn't stop, no matter how much I wish it would. Though I can't complain."

James chuckles, shaking his head. "Same old Emmett. Ever think about slowing down to invest in a different path?"

I roll my eyes. "Don't start. I get enough of that from Dad." The bar is crowded but not overly so—just enough noise to fill the spaces between words without drowning them out. It was good to sit, to let the day's weight slide off my shoulders for a while. We caught up on the usual—work, family, and mutual friends we hadn't seen in years.

James tells me about some big sale happening at his farm next week, something about clearing out old equipment. I half-listen, the beer working its way into my bloodstream, loosening me up just enough to relax but not enough to dull my focus. And then, as if he'd been waiting for the right moment, James shifts gears.

"So, I've been thinking," he begins, swirling his beer bottle.

"Dangerous words," I mutter, earning a laugh.

"I'm serious, man." He leans in a little, his expression losing its easy humor. "You've been talking about Ophelia and the teahouse nonstop. Don't even try to deny it."

"I—"

"Don't." He holds up a hand. "Let me finish."

I close my mouth, narrowing my eyes at him.

"Here's the thing," James continues. "I've been looking to downsize. The farm's a lot for me to handle on my own, and honestly, I'm ready for a change. I've been thinking about selling the farmhouse, the barn, the land—the whole thing."

I blink at him. "What does that have to do with—"

"Let me spell it out for you," James interrupts. "You take over the farm. The house, the land, all of it. I take over the teahouse and renovate it back into a regular home. I move into the teahouse, and you and Ophelia move into the farmhouse. Besides, it's just tucked behind the teahouse. She still gets her family creek and corner land, and it's still in Havenwood."

I stare at him like he's speaking a different language. "Wait —what? Me and Ophelia?"

James smirks. "Yeah. You and Ophelia. Don't play dumb, Emmett. It's always been her. Everyone knows it."

I open my mouth, then close it again, completely at a loss for words.

"Look," James says, his tone softening, "I'm not trying to put you on the spot. But I've been watching you dance around this for years. You care about her. Hell, you more than care about her. And I think she feels the same way about you, even if she's too scared to admit it."

My grip tightens around my beer bottle as his words sink in. He wasn't wrong—not entirely. Ophelia had been on my mind more than I cared to admit lately. But moving in together? Taking over a farm together? That was a whole different level of commitment.

"You're insane," I mutter, but the words lack conviction.

James laughs. "Maybe. But you're thinking about it, aren't you?"

I don't answer. I can't. Because, yeah, I am thinking about it. Thinking about her. Thinking about what it would mean to build something real, something lasting.

James claps me on the shoulder, his grin as infuriating as ever. "Just think it over, man. That's all I'm asking. The offer's there if you want it."

I nod, still too stunned to form a coherent response. My thoughts are tangled as we leave the bar and step out into the cool night air. James's words echo in my head, refusing to be ignored.

I barely remember the drive to Ophelia's. The roads were empty, the moon hanging low in the sky, and the radio played soft static as background noise. My hands grip the wheel tightly, knuckles pale in the glow of passing streetlights. James's words stuck to me like glue.

"It's always been her, man."

It wasn't just the solution he offered, though that was wild enough—more than I'd expected, more than I thought possible. It was how he said it, so matter-of-fact, like he'd known something about me before I figured it out myself.

I pull into her driveway, the gravel crunching under the tires. Her house is dark except for the soft flicker of light from the living room window. She might be asleep. Hell. I probably should've waited until tomorrow, but this couldn't wait.

Cutting the engine, I get out and stand there for a second, staring at her front door like it is a portal to something I can't fully understand yet. *Just tell her.* I walk up the steps and knock lightly, unsure if I want her to hear it or not.

It only takes a moment before the door creaks open. There she is—wrapped in a soft-looking cardigan, her hair a little messy, like she'd been curled up on the couch.

"Emmett?" she asks, her voice thick with sleep but warm. "It's late . . . Is everything okay?"

"I—yeah," I stammer, running a hand through my hair. "Sorry for showing up like this. I just . . . I needed to talk to you, Muffin."

She steps aside, motioning for me to come in. The warmth of her home wraps around me, the scent of lavender and something sweet hit me immediately.

"What's going on?" she asks, crossing her arms,

I hesitate, "I talked to my buddy James tonight. He's got an idea, and I think . . . I think it's a good one. But I wanted to tell you about it right away."

Shit . . . here we go. I shove my hands into my jacket pockets, letting the warmth of her home sink into my skin. Ophelia stands by the stairs, her eyes darting around like she wasn't sure if she wanted to sit down or run. Her brows are knit together, her lips slightly parting in a question that hasn't found its way out yet.

She stares at me, expectant but cautious. "What kind of idea?" she says slowly.

I hesitate for a moment, unsure of how to start. Then, with a deep breath, I dive in. "James is looking to downsize. He wants to sell his farm—the house, the barn, the land, all of it. And he thinks . . . well, he thinks you and I could take it over."

Her expression freezes for a beat before her brows shoot

up. "Take it over?" she echoes, her voice quieter but tinged with disbelief. "Like . . . together?"

The word 'together' hangs in the air, heavy and loaded. Together. It wasn't something I had fully processed until this moment, but there it was, staring me in the face.

"Yeah," I say, my voice steady despite the sudden pounding of my heart. "Together." Ophelia steps back, leaning against the wall as if she needs the support. Her arms drop to her sides, fingers curling against the fabric of her cardigan.

"I don't . . ." She shook her head. "I don't even know what to say, Emmett. This is a lot."

I want to hold her, but I resist. "I know it is," I say quickly, stepping closer but keeping enough space not to overwhelm her. "And I get that it's sudden, but hear me out, okay?"

She nods reluctantly, her eyes flicking up to meet mine.

"He'd live here . . ." I say, my voice gentler now. "Turn it back into a home. You wouldn't have to sell it to some stranger or worry about what happens to it. And the farm—it could be a fresh start for you. You've talked about wanting to grow more and expand your teas. That place could give you that and more."

Her lips part, and she draws in a shaky breath. "But . . . what about you? Why would you do all this?"

I step closer, feeling the air between us shift. "Because I want you to have what you deserve. Because you don't have to do this alone, Ophelia. And maybe . . . maybe I want to be part of it too."

She blinks, her lashes damp as her hands twist together nervously. "Emmett," she says softly, her voice cracking slightly. "This is—this is big. Bigger than just a business arrangement or a way to solve the teahouse problem. If we're talking about 'together,' what does that even mean? What are we?"

My heart skips at her words, and I take another step

forward, closing the space between us. "What do you want us to be?" I ask, my voice low and almost hesitant.

Her gaze flickers to the window, her cheeks flush. "I don't know. I mean, I've thought about it, but—"

I don't let her finish. "Ophelia," I interrupt gently, reaching out to take her hands in mine. They were cold, trembling slightly, but she didn't pull away. "I'm not good at this, but I'm gonna try, okay? Because you deserve someone who tries."

She looks up at me then, her eyes wide and searching.

"I want us to be something real," I say, my voice steady despite the thunder in my chest. "I want you to be mine, Ophelia. And I want to be yours if you'll have me."

Her breath catches, and she stares at me like she isn't sure if she's hearing me right. The silence stretches, each second feeling like a lifetime. Finally, she whispers, "You mean that?"

"With everything I've got, Little Lady," I say, squeezing her hands gently.

Her lips curve into the faintest smile, and the tension in her shoulders eases just a little. "I . . . I don't know what to say."

"Say you want me," I murmur, my voice low and rough as I step closer. My thumb brushes over her bottom lip, the softness of her skin sending a shockwave through me. Her tears glisten in the dim light, tracing delicate lines down her cheeks.

Ophelia's gaze meets mine, wide and trembling, like she is trying to decide whether to leap or stay grounded. Her lips part, a shaky breath slipping out as if the words she wants to say are caught in her throat. "I . . ." she starts, her voice breaking. Her fingers twist nervously in her cardigan, the knuckles white from the pressure.

I tilt my head, leaning in just enough to feel her breath against my skin. "Say it, Ophelia," I urge, my tone soft but insistent. "If you don't want me, tell me to stop. But if you do . . . if you need this as much as I do—say it."

She sucks in a breath, her shoulders rising and falling with the weight of whatever war was happening inside her. Then, slowly, her hand reaches out, trembling as it rests lightly on my chest. "I-I need you," she whispers, her voice barely audible but heavy with emotion. Her eyes flutter close as another tear slides down her cheek.

That's all I need to hear. My hand moves from her face to cradle the back of her neck, my fingers tangling gently in her hair. I pull her closer, closing the distance between us until there is no room for doubt or hesitation.

"Ophelia," I breathe, the weight of her name on my lips like a prayer. Then, I kissed her.

It wasn't rushed or desperate—it was slow and intentional like I needed her to feel every ounce of what I couldn't put into words. Her lips are soft and warm, trembling slightly as she leans into me. Her hands clutch the fabric of my shirt like it is the only thing anchoring her.

She tastes like the tea she loves so much, sweet and soothing, but there is something else—something uniquely her. A hint of fear, maybe, but it is overshadowed by how she sighs into the kiss, her body melting against mine.

My other hand finds her waist, holding her steady as I tilt my head, deepening the kiss just enough to let her know I'm not going anywhere. She whimpers softly, the sound shooting straight through me and making my grip tighten, anchoring us both in this moment.

When we finally pull apart, her cheeks are flushed, and her lips slightly swollen. Her eyes flutter open, and she looks up at me, dazed and breathless, her tears still glistening but forgotten.

"I . . ." she starts, her voice trembling as she tries to find the words.

I press my forehead against hers, my hand still at her waist. "Don't think," I murmur. "Just feel."

She nods slowly, her fingers still clutching my shirt as if

letting go would undo everything. "I feel . . . everything," she whispers.

"Good," I say softly, brushing my thumb over her cheek. "Because that's what you've got me feeling too."

Her lips curve into the faintest smile, and her tears finally dried as she relaxed into my arms. We're exactly where we're supposed to be.

Chapter Twenty-Two

OPHELIA

I wake to his warmth. I first notice the heat radiating from Emmett's body, his arm draping possessively over my waist. The morning sunlight filters through the curtains, painting the room in soft hues of gold and orange.

The gentle rise and fall of his chest presses against my back, and I can feel the steady rhythm of his breathing. My face flushes as reality sets in. Beneath the thin sheet tangled around us, I can feel his skin against mine, and the memory of the night before crashes over me like a wave.

My heart is pounding, thrilling, and terrifying me at once. I hold still for a moment, afraid that any movement might wake him. But then, as if sensing my hesitation, he stirs. His arm tightens around me, pulling me closer.

"Morning," his low, groggy voice rumbles, sending shivers down my spine. I swallow hard, my cheeks burning.

"Good morning," I manage, my voice softer than intended. His lips brush my shoulder, and I feel a smile against my skin. I turn to face him. His eyes, soft and unreadable, searched mine. His hair was messy from sleep, and his stubble was more pronounced in the morning light.

He looks . . . different like this. More vulnerable, somehow.

Something in the pit of my stomach comes alive. Not right now.

"You okay?" he whispers.

Was I okay? I am not sure how to answer that. My head was spinning, my emotions a tangled mess. I want to say yes, but the weight of everything—the kiss, the night, the unspoken promises—hang heavy between us. "I think so," I say finally, my words tentative. "Are you?"

He chuckles softly, his breath warm against my neck. "Better than okay," he says. "But I don't think you're convinced yet."

I face him, the sheet slipping slightly as I move. His eyes, soft and unreadable, searched mine. "It's just a lot," I admit, my voice barely above a whisper. "Everything feels so . . . big."

He looks at me and pushes his waist into me. "It is big."

I bite my lip. "Oh hush, that . . . that isn't what I mean."

His hand moves to cup my face. His thumb brushes over my cheek, grounding me. "We don't have to figure it all out right now. One step at a time, okay?"

I nod, but the lump in my throat doesn't go away. "It's just —this changes everything, doesn't it?"

He look saddens. "It doesn't have to," he says, his voice steady. "It can just . . . add to it. To us. If you want it to."

Us.

The word echoes in my mind, both comforting and terrifying. I hadn't let myself imagine an "us" for so long, and now here it was, staring me in the face.

"I'm scared," I admit, the words tumbling out before I could stop them.

"I know," he says gently. "But you don't have to be scared alone." His words wrap around me like a warm blanket. We lay there for hours, whispering about everything and nothing.

He tells me stories about his childhood, about when he tried to build a treehouse and fell out of the tree.

I laugh until tears stream down my face, and the weight on my chest lifts for a moment. But then, as the sunlight shifts and reality begins to creep back in, the heaviness returns.

"What happens now?" I ask, my voice barely audible. He looks at me, his expression serious.

"Well, we still have the festival coming, but after that . . . we would meet with James and get everything squared away." He looks at my lips and then back up. "If you still . . . need me."

He pulls me even closer, nearly on top of him. Emmett's hand tightens around mine, his knuckles turning white. His jaw is set, his eyes focusing on a point beyond me like he's bracing himself for something he can't quite face.

I turn onto my side, my hand resting against his cheek. "Emmett?"

His lips press into a thin line, and he shakes his head as if to push whatever is brewing back down. But I can see it—his chest rising and falling faster, his brows knit together, his Adam's apple bobbing as he swallowed hard.

"Talk to me," I say softly.

"I'm fine," he mutters, his voice gruff.

"No, you're not." My thumb brushes over his cheek, and I feel the faintest tremble beneath my touch. "You don't have to hold it in. Not with me."

He closes his eyes tightly, his breath shuddering as he exhales. "Ophelia, I don't. . . I can't."

"Yes, you can," I say, my voice steady but tender. "You're safe here. Whatever it is, let it out."

His chest heaves, and I watch as the walls he always kept so carefully in place start to crack. "I'm just—" His voice breaks, and he drags a hand through his hair, his frustration palpable. "It's a lot, Ophelia. You, the teahouse, everything I want for us, everything I'm afraid I'll mess up. I want to do it right. I want to be what you deserve, but I don't know if I can—"

Tears slip down his cheeks, unbidden and raw. He turns his face away, ashamed, but I won't let him hide.

"Emmett." I guide his face back to mine, my hands firm but gentle. "It's okay. You don't have to be perfect. You don't have to do it all alone. I'm here and need you to let go of this weight you're carrying."

He stares at me, his eyes glassy and full of pain. "I don't know how."

"Yes, you do," I say softly. "You've been holding it in for so long, but you don't have to anymore. Let it go. I've got you— no—we have each other now."

The dam breaks. His head falls to my shoulder as his body shakes with sobs. I wrap my arms around him, holding him tightly as years of grief, fear, and frustration pour out of him. I stroke his hair, whispering soothing words as he clings to me like a lifeline.

"It's okay," I murmur. "Let it out. You're safe." Minutes pass, or maybe hours—I am not sure. All I know is that I won't let go until he is ready.

Finally, his breathing begins to steady, and he lifts his head, his face red and tear-streaked. He stares at me with such raw vulnerability that it makes my heart ache.

"I'm sorry," he says, his voice hoarse.

"For what?" I asked gently.

"For falling apart like that. For . . . everything." I shake my head, cupping his face in my hands. "Don't apologize. You needed that. We both do, sometimes."

Heyes are searching mine. "You're. . . incredible," he says, his voice thick with emotion.

"I'm just me," I say with a small smile.

"And that's perfect, Mossgrove," he says, his lips curving into the faintest smile.

I brush my lips against his in a soft kiss, full of promise. "I need you, Emmett," I whisper.

A deep growl rumbles from him, low and primal, as his arms wrap around me to pull me onto his lap. His hands grip my hips, and his eyes blaze with intensity.

"And I want you," I add, my voice trembling.

"Perfect, Little Lady," he says, his voice rough with desire and affection. He holds me close, his hands steadying me as he looks at me like I am the most precious thing in the world. Then, his voice softens, and the weight of his following words make my heart stop. "I plan to marry you, Ophelia Dawn Mossgrove."

My breath hitches, and our eyes lock.

"And . . ." I pause, my lips curving into a shaky smile. "I plan to say yes, Emmett Davidius Sterling."

He grins wide, his hands sliding up to cradle my face as he tugs me down for a kiss that is anything but gentle. It is fierce, consuming, and full of every unspoken promise we'd made to each other. We still had so much to do . . . but I knew it was going to be okay.

Chapter Twenty-Three

EMMETT

The days leading up to the festival were nothing short of chaos. For the past four days, I'd been glued to my phone, juggling calls from vendors who couldn't find their booth assignments, artists on the brink of canceling because they doubted their work, and volunteers needing direction.

I'd walked the grounds more times than I could count, double and triple-checking that the stage was set up correctly, weatherproofed, and ready for performances. I am running on fumes.

Today is more of the same. By lunchtime, I'd already reviewed lists of sellables from every vendor, coaxed nervous first-timers into staying the course, and fielded at least a hundred calls from my dad. Apparently, he can't stop micromanaging, even from his own plans.

"It'll be fine, Dad," I mutter into the phone for what feels like the tenth time, trying to keep my voice level. "Yes, I'm sure they've double-checked the electrical hookups. No, I don't need you to come down and inspect them." Sighing, I end the call, resisting the urge to toss my phone onto the nearest table.

"Trouble with your old man again?" I see Ophelia approaching, her steps brisk but graceful as always. She has a piece of paper and an amused twinkle in her eye. "I heard you're the guy who has to approve this, cowboy," she teases, sliding the paper toward me.

I flip it over and stare at the blank page. "Mossgrove, is this a joke?"

She glances around, lowering her voice as she leans in. "I haven't decided what to do yet, Emmett. Keep your voice down," she hisses, her expression sharp but tinged with exasperation.

The thumping in my temples turns into a full-on headache. I got it—Ophelia had been just as swamped as I was. This was her first festival in years, and I could tell the pressure was getting to her.

I pinch the bridge of my nose. "I need it soon, Muffin. I've got to turn in the final permits tomorrow."

She flashes a grin, one of those quick, mischievous smiles that soften the edges of her stress. "First thing tomorrow, I promise," she says, already retreating before I could argue.

"Ophelia—" I firmly say.

"Goodnight, Emmett!" she calls over her shoulder, vanishing into the evening crowd. I look around, realizing no one is waiting. The vendors had packed up for the day. The last rays of sunlight is bathing the cobblestone streets in a warm glow. For the first time in hours, it is quiet. The thought of my bed nearly makes me groan out loud.

I grab my bag, check the clipboard one last time, and head home, exhaustion pulling at every step. The festival isn't even here, and I already feel like I ran a marathon. But it would be worth it—at least, I hoped so.

At night, I lay in bed, staring at the ceiling as the hum of my thoughts drown out the world outside. The weight of the festival, the endless lists, and the string of phone calls ran on a loop in my head.

But one thought keeps circling back, louder than the rest: Ophelia.

I replayed her flustered look earlier, how she handed me that blank piece of paper with a sheepish grin. I could see the stress she tried to hide, the tension in her shoulders when she thought no one was watching. But there was something else, too—a spark, a determination beneath the surface that never seemed to dim.

I turn onto my side, letting out a deep breath. The room felt too warm, my body too restless, and I can't shake the feeling that she is still here with me somehow, her presence lingering in the air. Her voice echoes in my head. That teasing *"cowboy,"* the playful grin she flashes before disappearing.

A low ache builds in my chest, spreading through me, and I let out a quiet, frustrated sigh. My hand drifts down, a hesitant touch as I close my eyes and let the image of her fill my thoughts.

Her hair catching the light, the curve of her lips when she smiles, and her eyes soft as she looks at me like I am someone worth seeing. I exhale slowly, the tension in my body giving way as my mind gave into the fantasy of her—

Ophelia—here with me—her warmth chasing away the day's chaos. For a brief moment, everything else fades: the festival, the stress, the relentless to-do list. All that remains is the thought of her, vivid and unyielding.

When it's over, I lay still, the room's silence settling over me again. My breath slow, my body relaxed, but my thoughts didn't stop. If anything, they linger longer, tracing the edges of something I am not sure I want to admit. The buzzing of my phone pulls me back to reality. I glance at the screen, sighing when I see "Dad."

"What now?" I answer, barely concealing my exasperation.

"Good to hear your cheerful voice," Dad replies, his tone dripping with sarcasm. "Listen, we need a final count for the parade lineup by tomorrow. Did you follow up with the florists about decorating the floats?"

I pinch the bridge of my nose. "Yes, Dad. *Emerald's Blooms* are all set, and they're coordinating with *Whiskers & Wool* for some cutesy pet float."

"Good, good," he says, and I can hear the shuffle of papers on his end. "And the bakery?"

"Also, good. Ophelia's handling the treats."

"Well, excuse me for double-checking," he shoots back. Then, after a pause, he adds, "Have you stopped by to see her yet? Talked to her about what she's planning?"

I hesitate. I knew she didn't have the details of her menu yet. "Not yet."

"Why not?"

"Let me handle it. I haven't had time," I mutter, taking the blame.

"That's not an excuse." His tone shifts slightly, less the commanding mayor and more the concerned father. "You've got to make time, Emmett. Not just for the festival but for yourself."

"I'm fine," I say quickly, although the words feel hollow.

"Are you?" he asks, his voice softening. The silence stretches for a moment before he continues. "Emmett, I've been doing some thinking."

"Uh-oh," I tease, trying to lighten the mood.

He ignores it. "The post office . . . don't worry about it anymore."

"What?" My heart sinks. Not this again.

"You heard me. Forget it," he says, the words calm but firm. "I've got someone else covering the job now. It's time you stop holding onto something not meant for you anymore."

I blink, his words catching me off guard. "Are you sure?"

"Don't question me, kid." There was a hint of a smile in his tone. "Look, I get it. You're still figuring things out. But the post office isn't part of that picture anymore. You've got bigger things to focus on—like this festival and . . ." he pauses, letting the weight of his following words settle. ". . . whatever comes next for you."

I swallow hard, not sure what to say.

"I see it, Emmett," he continues, his voice gentle. "You've got a dream you're chasing, even if you don't fully know what it looks like. And maybe part of it has something to do with that tea shop on the edge of town."

"Dad . . ."

"Havenwood's always been here for you, but maybe it's time for you to be here for yourself—for once."

For a moment, I didn't know what to say. Then I nod, even though he can't see me. "Thanks, Dad."

"Don't thank me yet," he says, the smile audible in his voice. "You've still got a festival to pull off. Now, go. And don't make me call you again."

"Yeah, right," I say with a small laugh. But as the line goes quiet, I find myself laying there, the phone still in hand, feeling lighter than I had in weeks. Maybe Dad is right. Maybe it's time to stop holding back.

Chapter Twenty-Four

OPEHLIA

The morning sunlight spills across the kitchen, illuminating the stacks of notebooks, loose recipes, and ingredient lists sprawling across the table.

My kitchen, usually my haven, feels more like a battlefield today.

The Fall Festival was just a single night away, and I still hadn't finalized the menu for the teahouse booth. Everything else, with the help of Emmett, was done, but this final thing—the most important thing—was still not done.

I stare at the blank page in my notebook, the pen hovering above it like a sword I am too scared to wield. My mind races with possibilities, each more elaborate than the last, but none are right. I need the menu to be perfect—not just for the festival but for me.

Pulling in a deep breath, I start with the baked goods. Those were the easy part—or so I thought. First, the scones. My hands move methodically, measuring flour, sugar, baking powder, and salt. I cut in the cold butter with practiced preci-sion, as my mother had taught me years ago.

The pastry cutter scraping against the bowl is oddly soothing, grounding me in the moment. "Blueberry lemon," I murmur, jotting the flavor in my notebook.

The muffins are next. They are classic, dependable, and one of my best sellers. I want something warm and comforting, something that screams autumn. Pumpkin spice muffins are a no-brainer. I add a pinch of cinnamon and nutmeg, the spices perfuming the air as I mix the batter.

The cookies are trickier. Everyone loves chocolate chip cookies, but the festival calls for something special. I thumb through my recipe cards until I find one that makes me smile: brown butter maple pecan cookies. They are delightful, nutty, and perfectly seasonal.

I jot down the selections and move on to the teas. This part should have been easier, but as I stare at my jars of dried herbs and tea leaves, doubt creeps in like an unwelcome guest.

"Sterling," I whisper, my eyes landing on the mystery blend I'd been perfecting for weeks. It was a rich, warm blueberry muffin tea—sweet yet subtle, with hints of vanilla and almond. I hadn't named it yet, but I thought of Emmett whenever I brewed a pot. His quiet strength, his steadfastness, how he looked at me like I was the only thing in the world that mattered.

I scribble the name "Sterling" in my notebook, then circle it twice for good measure.

As I work, the weight of it all begins to press down on me. The festival, the menu, the expectations—it feels like too much. My hands tremble as I reach for a jar of dried lavender, knocking it over in the process. The sound of glass shattering on the floor is the breaking point. Tears well up in my eyes, blurring the mess at my feet.

Not again . . . not this again. *Please.*

"I can't do this," I whisper to the empty kitchen. "I can't."

I sink onto the floor, my back against the cabinets, and let the tears fall. For a few minutes, I let myself feel overwhelmed by the fear and the crushing weight of perfectionism. But then, a small voice inside me whispers, "You've been through worse. You've climbed higher mountains than this."

I wipe my face with the sleeve of my sweater and take a shaky breath. One step at a time, I tell myself. Just one step at a time. There is no more running.

I stand, sweep up the broken glass, and start over. By late afternoon, the menu is finally complete:

- Blueberry Lemon Scones
- Pumpkin Spice Muffins
- Brown Butter Maple Pecan Cookies
- Winter Tea Blends: Cranberry Spice, Vanilla Chai, and Sterling

I stare at the list. Pride swelling in my chest despite the lingering exhaustion. It isn't perfect, but it's mine. Just as I'm about to call it a day, the back door creaks open.

I see Emmett leaning against the doorframe, his hat tilted low over his eyes.

"Smells good in here, Little Lady," he says, his gaze sweeping over the table.

"Thanks, Cowboy," I reply, brushing a strand of hair from my face.

He steps inside, his boots clicking against the tile.

"How's it coming along?" I hesitate, the anxiety still lurking at the edges of my mind.

"It's. . . coming." He studies me for a moment, his brow furrowing. "You okay?"

I nod, forcing a smile. "Just a long day."

His hand brushes mine as he steals a stray blueberry on the counter. The slight touch was enough to steady me.

"You're gonna knock it outta the park," he says, popping the berry into his mouth.

I laugh softly, the tension easing just a bit. "You think so?"

"Know so," he replies, his voice firm. I open my mouth to say something, but his hands are on my waist before I can. His touch is warm, firm, grounding—like he's determined to hold me in this moment, where the world outside the kitchen didn't exist.

I let out a soft gasp as he tilts my chin up, his eyes searching mine with an intensity I don't expect. It's sudden, a forceful meeting of lips, but not harsh. In fact, it's gentle and hungry all at once. His fingers cup the back of my neck, pulling me in deeper, and the warmth of his breath mixes with mine.

I respond instinctively, my hands sliding up to his chest, gripping his shirt as if I need something to hold on to. The kiss deepens. My heart races. The heat of his body pressing against mine ignites a fire I hadn't realized was smoldering.

He tugs me closer, his lips soft against mine, and I can't help but melt into him.

"Ophelia," he breathes, his voice thick with desire. "I've wanted this, I've wanted you. All week . . ."

The words hit me like a wave. There's no teasing, no hesitation—just the raw truth in his voice. It makes my insides tighten with need, and I realize that everything I had been feeling, every flutter of my heart when I saw him, was suddenly impossible to ignore. He leans down again, this time with a slow, deliberate kiss.

I let him guide me, his hands moving down to my waist as he presses us up against the counter. The heat between us intensifies, my body responding before my mind can catch up. The moment was too much, too quick, and yet it was everything I'd been holding back.

I don't want to stop. I don't want to pull away. His hands slide beneath the hem of my shirt, and I feel his warmth against my skin, sending a ripple of electricity through me.

"Emmett," I breathe, my voice barely a whisper, but it's enough to make him pause.

He looks at me, his gaze darkened, but there's a softness there, too—an understanding that made my heart race even faster. "Do you want this, Ophelia?" he whispers.

"Y-yes," I shakily say. And then, with a deep, almost desperate kiss, he lifts me into his arms, carrying me toward the table. The world outside the kitchen, the festival's worries, the doubts plaguing me all week—they all faded into the background. It's just him and me and the storm we are both trying to navigate.

His lips move from mine, trailing kisses along my neck and down to my shoulder. His hands grip the edge of my shirt, pulling it over my head. Every movement is like a promise—one that makes my heart race and my mind spin. He is gentle but firm, taking his time with me, exploring every inch of my skin with his lips and hands, reminding me of all the things I had been afraid to let myself feel.

When he finally looks at me, his eyes burning with desire, he whispers, "You're everything I've wanted, Ophelia. You better run up those stairs, Little Lady," he says, his voice low and full of challenge.

I freeze for a second, my heart pounding in surprise. I'm still partially naked on the kitchen table, my cheeks flush, eyes wide.

"W-what?" I stutter, unsure if I heard him right.

His gaze darkens, and he leans in a little closer. "Or I will take you right here, right now," he growls, his tone sending a thrill down my spine. I can't help the laugh that bubbles up. I shake my head, still grinning.

"Come get me, cowboy." Without thinking, I spring up and ran toward the stairs as fast as my legs can carry me. Laughter spills from my lips—freer and lighter than I've felt in years.

"Oh, this is gonna be fun," I mutter as I dart up the stairs.

Behind me, I hear him shout, "Here I come!"

My breath quickens. *Oh shit.*

Chapter Twenty-Five

EMMETT

I step back from Ophelia's booth, taking in the final touches with a sense of quiet satisfaction. The tables are arranged just right, the linens crisp and inviting, and the vintage-style baskets we spent hours filling are now stacked with the perfect selection of muffins, scones, and cookies.

The teacups, delicate and elegant, catch the first light of the morning sun, their soft glow adding a touch of magic to the scene. Ophelia's booth has become a cozy little world of its own, every detail reflecting the warmth and charm she brings to everything she touches. It's as warm and inviting as she is, and I can't help but admire how effortlessly she's turned it into a space that feels like home.

I linger for a moment longer, feeling the surge of pride I've grown accustomed to whenever I look at her. She's worked so hard for this, and I've been here, watching her grow more confident with each passing day, more willing to embrace a future she once thought was out of reach.

Today feels like a first step forward for both of us, not just for her. I glance around the festival grounds, the bustle of activity slowly picking up as the townsfolk trickle in. The air is filled with the intoxicating scents of fresh bread, coffee, and caramelized sugar, mixing with the crisp smell of fallen leaves that cling to the autumn air. It's the kind of morning that makes you want to take it all in and savor it, like the first sip of a warm cup of tea on a chilly day.

I wander through a few other booths, exchanging greetings with vendors and making small talk. Familiar faces wave as I walk by, and I'm reminded of the community that has shaped me. Something about Havenwood—its tight-knit feel and shared history— keeps pulling me back, even when I thought I had outgrown it.

Here, I'm not just another face in the crowd. I'm part of something bigger, something that's always been in the blood of this town. Eventually, I make my way to the far end of the market, toward a quiet corner near the woods. It's secluded, tucked away from the hustle of the main grounds, a perfect spot for what I've set up.

I take a moment to adjust a small model barn next to an old oak tree. A humble setup meant to honor the past. A couple of stools sit at the edges, and I carefully arrange thlike mue small assortment of auto parts I brought. It's not flashy. It's simple. It's a tribute. The sign reads: *Willie's Auto Parts, In Remembrance.*

I pause momentarily, my fingers brushing along the table's edge. A familiar ache stirs in my chest. Ophelia's dad was a man of few words, but something about his quiet confidence made you feel like you could ask him anything. His shop was more than just a business—it was a place of legend in this town. I spent hours there, learning, listening, and watching him tinker with bikes and cars. His hands, calloused from years of work, would piece together broken parts like they were puzzles, the same way he pieced together people's lives.

He never quite got to see how the world was changing, but I know he would've been proud to see this town come together like it has. I pull out an acrylic frame I set aside, carefully placing it on the table. It's a photo of Ophelia and her dad standing before one of his vintage motorcycles, his arm around her shoulders. Her face lit up with the brightest smile.

That smile—it's something I think about often, especially in the quiet moments before I fall asleep at night. It's the same smile I saw when she agreed to give us a chance when she opened up to me. A smile full of hope. A smile full of trust.

I admire the photo, my chest tightening with the weight of my feelings. I hope this small tribute will touch her heart like nothing else can. Last night, I called her mom and arranged for her to run the booth, keeping it a secret from Ophelia.

I know how much she misses her dad. This—this small gesture—will remind her of all the good things her father represented, of the legacy he left behind. With that done, I head back to Ophelia's booth, a small rush of excitement in my chest. The festival's energy is picking up now, families wandering through, the sound of chatter and music filling the air.

I catch a glimpse of her as I approach. She is still busy at work, arranging the last of her tea blends and placing the colorful tins in neat rows.

"Busy day?" I tease, my voice light as I step up to her. She looks up, offering me a warm smile.

"I've still got a few things to do," she replies, her fingers brushing over a stack of cups. "But it's coming together. Slowly but surely."

I step behind the booth, admiring the spread she's created. Her famous scones and muffins are perfectly golden and inviting, and the scent of baked goods fills the air. Her tea collection is exquisite—each blend thoughtfully chosen, each tin a small work of art.

My eyes move across the table until I pause at one particular tin. My fingers brush over the label.

"Sterling?" I chuckle, lifting the tin in my hand. "Is this a joke, Little Lady?"

Her eyes flicker to meet mine, and I can see the faintest

flush creep across her cheeks. "What? You don't think your name would make a good tea blend?"

I laugh softly, the amusement evident in my voice. "What kind of blend is it?"

"It's a muffin-tea blend," she says, her smile widening as she watches me. "I thought it might be fitting. You're always offering your 'help,' and now you've become a blend of my life."

Her words catch me off guard, and a tightness forms in my chest. I stare at the tin for a moment longer, the weight of her affection settling deep inside me. I feel it—the pull, the warmth between us, the connection that's grown over time. "Well, I think it's perfect," I say softly, my voice steady. "But not as perfect as you."

Her eyes meet mine, and for a brief second, everything else disappears. I step closer to her, feeling the distance between us vanish as I look down at her with a smile that says everything I can't put into words.

"I love you," she softly whispers against my chest. *She loves me.*

"And I love you," I whisper back, kissing the top of her head.

The festival is in full swing. Laughter rings out across the grounds, the chatter of families and children filling the air. But my focus is still on Ophelia. She's busy moving between customers, explaining the nuances of her tea blends, and arranging her baked goods with the same precision and care she's put into everything today.

But I can see the subtle signs of tension creeping in. The way her hands move too quickly and her gaze darts around the crowd like she's trying to juggle it all at once. I can't help but feel like she's on the edge and needs a break. I glance at the booth behind her—the small tribute to her dad waiting patiently for her to see it.

I'm excited, but I don't want to overwhelm her. She's been working so hard, and I know she deserves this small gift, even if it's just a moment of remembering. I approach her carefully, brushing my fingers against hers as I lean in slightly.

"Hey," I say softly, my voice almost drowned out by the hum of the festival. She looks up at me, her smile warm but weary.

"Hey . . ." Her voice holds a quiet vulnerability as if she's waiting for me to give her some reassurance.

"I was thinking," I begin, my voice light but purposeful. "Maybe you could use a break. How about we take a walk? I want to show you something."

Her gaze flickers over her booth, the day clearly pressing on her shoulders. She hesitates for a moment, then nods, giving in to the invitation in my voice. "Alright," she agrees, a smile tugging at the corners of her mouth. "But only if you promise to make it quick. Things are about to get busy again, Emmett."

"I promise," I reply, gently taking her hand. The moment our fingers intertwine, a calm settles in my chest. We walk together, the sounds of the festival fading behind us as we move toward the quieter part of the grounds. The air is warm, filled with the hum of conversations and the scent of caramel apples and fresh-cut flowers. There's a lightness in the air today that hasn't been there in a long time, and I find myself savoring it.

We pass a booth with a woman selling hand-knitted scarves, the soft colors of the yarn catching the sunlight. Ophelia stops to admire one, running her fingers along the threads. "These are beautiful," she murmurs, her eyes alight with appreciation.

I watch her, wondering how long it's been since she genuinely looked at something like this with that kind of wonder.

"Maybe you should get one," I say, nudging her gently. "It'd look good on you."

She shoots me a smile but shakes her head. "I have enough scarves, I think," she whispers, but I can see her desire for just one more. We keep walking, passing by more vendors. A man at a fruit stand offers us a small sample of strawberries dipped in chocolate, and Ophelia's eyes light up as she bites into one.

"That's amazing," she says with a satisfied grin. "You should try one."

I chuckle, grabbing one for myself. The sweetness is almost overwhelming, but I can't deny it's delicious.

"Not bad," I admit. Next, we come across a tea stand, and Ophelia's eyes immediately sparkle. She steps up to the counter, chatting with the vendor, a woman with bright red hair and a warm smile. I'm content to stand back and let her enjoy the conversation, watching her face light up as the woman pours a sample of sweet tea into a small cup. Ophelia takes a sip, and her eyes widen.

"This is incredible," she says, turning to me. "You have to try this."

I raise an eyebrow, amused. "I thought you were the tea expert."

She grins. "I am, but I can't even make something like this." I take a sip myself, and I can't help but agree. It's sweet, but not overwhelmingly so, with just a hint of citrus that balances out the flavor perfectly.

"Okay, I'll admit it's good," I say.

As we move away from the booth, I notice a fried food stand just a few feet away. A mischievous grin spreads across my face.

"Hey, Ophelia, want to try a fried Oreo?"

She looks at me like I've lost my mind. "Fried Oreo? That sounds . . ." She trails off, raising an eyebrow, clearly unsure. Her turn is over. Now she must try something I like.

I hand her a plate with the fried Oreo, eager to watch her reaction. She takes a tentative bite, and as she does, I lean in to make a joke, but my hand slips. The Oreo tumbles off the plate and lands with a soft thud on the ground.

We both stare at the sad, battered cookie for a moment. Then, without warning, Ophelia bursts into laughter—loud, carefree, the kind of laugh so infectious I can't help but join in.

My stomach tightens from laughing so much, and I feel a warmth spread through me that's not from the sun.

"I—oh my god," she gasps between giggles, wiping tears from her eyes. "I can't believe you dropped it!"

I'm grinning like an idiot, my own laughter ringing in my ears. "I swear I didn't mean to."

We both stand there for a moment, laughing until our sides ache. Just me, Ophelia, and the fried Oreo I'll never live down. When we finally reach the corner by the oak tree, I stop and step aside.

"Here we are, Little Lady," I say, my heart thumping in my chest. Ophelia's eyes scan the booth, confusion briefly crossing her face as she takes it all in. Then, her gaze falls on the sign.

"Willie's Auto Parts, In Remembrance." She reads the words aloud, her voice soft and reverent. She steps closer, her fingers brushing the table's edge, where the old auto parts are carefully arranged. Her breath catches in her throat. Her expression softens, a mixture of nostalgia and a deeper sadness that tugs at my heart.

"This is . . . this is beautiful, Emmett," she whispers, her voice thick with emotion. "I never expected you to do something like this."

I approach her, my voice low as I try to describe the

emotion flooding me. "I wanted to do something for you, Ophelia. For your dad. He meant so much to this town."

She looks up at me, her eyes glistening with unshed tears. "Thank you," she whispers, her voice barely audible. "This . . . this is exactly what I needed."

I take her into a hug, squeezing her tight. "He'd be so proud of you, Ophelia," I cup her face, "So damn proud."

I kiss her forehead as she melts into my arms. She takes one last look before returning to her booth, where a line has formed.

She turns back to look at me and grins, "Come on, Cowboy."

Gladly.

Chapter Twenty-Six

OPHELIA

My booth felt alive. The comforting rhythm of the sales, the clinking of coins, and the chattering of patrons all wrap me in a bubble of cozy chaos.

I ran my hands along the smooth wood of the counter, fidgeting with the edge of a napkin as another customer approaches. It's my way of keeping calm. Anxiety always seems to creep up on me in moments like this, but I learned how to manage it over the last few weeks. Just breathe. Keep moving.

A smile always helps, too. I offer my brightest one to the woman stepping up to the booth. "Can I help you with anything today?" I ask, trying to keep my voice steady.

"Oh, yes, please!" she says, scanning the display. "How much for the muffins?"

"Two for five," I reply, careful to keep my hands from shaking as I wrap up her order. As I hand her the bag, I feel my shoulders relax. The weight of my anxiety lighter for the moment. It isn't gone, but I can handle it. I can.

I lift my head just in time to see three small faces peeking over the counter. The homeschool co-op regulars. A little boy with messy brown hair, a girl in pigtails, and a slightly older boy with a mischievous grin.

"Muffins!" the little boy, Theodore, says, his eyes wide with excitement. I hand each of them a single muffin, but just as I turn around to discard the wrappers, the muffins are gone.

"Can we have more?" Olivia, the girl, asks, her fingers tapping on the counter, a wide grin on her face.

Mason, the oldest, who couldn't have been more than eight, giggled. "More, please? You're really good at making them!"

I chuckle, feeling my heart warm. These kids were adorable. "More, huh?" I ask. "You've already had one."

They nod vigorously, their faces so earnest it is almost impossible to say no.

"Well, how about this," I say, leaning down a little so they could hear me. "If you can tell me which of you has the biggest sweet tooth, I'll give you an extra muffin. Deal?"

They all glanced at each other, and for a split second, I think they might burst into a full-on debate about who was the biggest sweet tooth. But then Mason raises his hand. "I do!" he declares proudly.

"Well then, I think we can make an exception," I say, reaching into the basket of fresh muffins.

"Yay!" they cheer together, bouncing on their heels in unison. I hand them each another muffin, feeling a little flutter of joy at their excitement. "But remember," I add with a smile, "we don't want to spoil dinner."

They giggled and ran off, their laughter trailing behind them. I feel a soft warmth wash over me as I return to my work. The innocence of those children, the pure joy in their eyes, took me back to when I was their age. I remembered running through the house, stealing cookies off the cooling rack as Mom baked. She'd always catch me with crumbs on my face, but she never scolded me. She'd just laugh and let me have one.

I pause for a moment, remembering those days. It feels like such a different world now, but that same comfort—being around food and creating something that brings people happiness—is still here. I love seeing others enjoy what I make, and the simplicity of it is everything. I don't have to think too hard to know that this is where I belong—this booth, these muffins, the people around me.

Just then, the parents of the kids appear, a little out of breath as they catch up with their children. "I'm so sorry," the mother says, wringing her hands. "I hope they didn't take too many."

I wave it off, smiling. "No need to apologize. They were wonderful customers. Honestly, I've got plenty of muffins to spare."

The father chuckles, shaking his head. "I don't know how you do it. I can barely get them to stop eating at home."

I shrug, still smiling. "It's all part of the fun. Watching kids enjoy something so simple is one of the best parts of this."

The mother smiles back at me. "Well, thank you again. You've made their day."

I watch them walk away, the children already munching happily on their treats. I turn back to my booth, wiping my hands on my apron. And if nothing else, I'd always have my muffins and children's laughter to remind me that life—simple and sweet—was enough.

The evening sky deepens into a dusky purple, and the last festival-goers trickle out of the park. My booth is quiet now, except for the soft rustle of the wind through the trees and the distant murmur of the town winding down after a long, bustling day. The sun is set behind the trees, casting a golden glow on everything as I stand behind the counter, wiping down the last of the trays.

I take a deep breath, letting the day settle around me. It was a good day. A busy day.

The kind of day where I felt useful and alive, even though my feet ached and my shoulders were stiff from standing. I can't help but hum as I now clean down the table with the cloth, swaying a little with the rhythm. Everything's finally winding down, and I am ready to call it a night.

The final remnants of baked goods wrapped, the tea jars packed away, and the leftover napkins folded neatly. With a small sigh of satisfaction, I tuck everything into the wooden crate. The familiar weight of it grounds me. I glance around at the empty booth, feeling a sense of pride.

I did it. The booth was a success, and I made it through the festival without losing my mind. I hadn't let my anxiety take over. I hadn't retreated into my shell. I managed to keep it together, even if just for a day.

A soft tune slips from my lips as I hum the song I'd been singing earlier, a little off-key but full of joy. I dance around the booth, swaying with the motion as I tidy up.

The moment has a certain sweetness, as if the world slowed just enough to let me catch my breath. I grab the last crates and carefully stack them on the wooden cart that would carry everything to my truck, parked a few feet away. The air is crisp now, with just a hint of chill, but the glow from the streetlamps warms the path. As I push it towards my truck, the cart tires click along the cobblestone. I am still singing to myself, my feet light despite the burden of the crates. Like a private celebration. Just me and the night.

The distant clink of my truck's tailgate echoes in the quiet space as I carefully pack everything into the back of my truck.

"Hey, you forgot something."

I freeze, hearing the familiar voice before I even turn

around. My heart does a little flip in my chest, and I smile before even seeing him.

"Forgot something?" I ask, glancing over my shoulder. Emmett stands a few feet away, his arms crossed, a smirk playing on his lips. The last of the lights from the festival casts him in a warm glow, making the moment feel like some kind of movie scene. I raise an eyebrow, confused. "I don't think I forgot anything. I've got everything packed up."

He shakes his head, his grin widening. "No, I mean . . . you forgot me."

The words take a moment to sink in, but when they do, I blink and laugh softly, a little breathless. "Oh. You . . . you're right. I did forget you."

His eyes soften, and that playful smirk fades into something more genuine. He steps closer, a slow stride that seems to pull me in even further, like he knows the effect he has on me. "I figured I'd walk you back to your place. The night's still young. I can come back and get your truck."

I glance at my truck, feeling the warm hum of the engine waiting for me. The thought of going back to my quiet home alone feels different now. With Emmett here, standing so close, everything is less solitary.

"Yeah," I say, finding my voice, the uncertainty gone. "I think I'd like that."

Emmett chuckled softly, his eyes crinkling at the corners as he met my gaze. "Good. I'm not done for the night yet, either. I'll walk you home."

I take the keys and lock the truck as I turn to Emmett, who is already starting to walk toward the path leading home. "Lead the way," I say, my voice steady now. I feel him lace soft fabric around my shoulder. I peer down—the scarf. I don't say a word . . . I just follow him into the night.

Chapter Twenty-Seven

EMMETT

It's been a few weeks since Ophelia and I broke the news to everyone—my parents, my sister, and even Florence and her mom. I was ready for some resistance, maybe a little pushback, but instead, I got hugs, smiles, and even a knowing look from my dad that felt like a quiet blessing.

Thank God. To my surprise, everyone was on board. Mom was already planning to bring casseroles to the farm "just in case." Florence immediately offered to help Ophelia brainstorm ideas for the garden.

And Dad?

He simply said, "About time."

Which was his way of saying he approved and to be honest, I am glad they all did, because . . . I wouldn't be able to handle any pushback right now. We need all the support we can get. With all the big conversations behind us, we are packing up and getting ready for the next step. The house was starting to feel like it wasn't mine anymore, and instead of sadness, all I feel is relief.

"You know, if you stare at that box any harder, it's going to catch fire," Ophelia teases from the doorway. There is a dust smudge on her cheek, probably from the attic, where she'd been helping pack my old things.

"I was just debating whether this box should go to the farm or straight to the dumpster," I shoot back.

"Which box is it?" She walks in, peering over my shoulder.

"The one with my old college textbooks," I admit.

"Oh, definitely the dumpster," she says with mock seriousness. "Unless you're planning to start tutoring calculus on the side?"

"Hey, those books were expensive," I argue, though I already know she's right. "Besides, you never know when I might need to brush up on advanced physics."

She gives me a look that says, *you're ridiculous.* "The only physics you care about is how fast you can rebuild an engine. Let's be real."

"Fair," I admit with a grin. "But if we're throwing out useless stuff, what about that box of teapots you're bringing?"

Her eyes narrow playfully. "Those teapots are vintage. And they all serve a purpose."

"Yeah, decoration," I tease.

She huffs, crossing her arms. "Says the man with a box labeled: *Random Wrenches.*"

"Hey, those are collectibles," I say, throwing her words back at her. She rolls her eyes, but a laugh gives her away.

"Alright, you win. For now." I pick up one of the boxes, hefting it onto the counter.

"Speaking of winning, I've got an idea about how we can make this whole move even better."

"Oh?" She tilts her head, her curiosity immediately piqued.

"With the money from selling my house," I begin, "I want to renovate the barn at the farm, Little Lady."

Her eyebrows shoot up. "The barn? The one with the sagging roof and the family of raccoons?" She fidgets with her thumbs.

"Yeah, that one." I can't help but laugh. "Think about it. We turn it into a proper teahouse. You've been saying you want to separate work and home, and this would give you the space to do it. You could have your dream setup right there on the property."

She stares at me for a moment, and I start to wonder if I've overstepped. But then her expression softens, and her eyes begin to shimmer.

"You'd really do that?" she asks, her voice barely above a whisper.

"Of course, I would. You've built something amazing with the teahouse, Ophelia. I want you to have a space to grow it without feeling like you're losing yourself." I trap her against the counter playfully, letting my smile widen. "Plus, it's selfish, really. I like the idea of sitting on the porch and watching you work your magic over there."

She laughs, and it's the kind of laugh that feels like sunlight breaking through a cloudy day. "You're ridiculous, Emmett Sterling."

"But in a good way, right?"

"The best way," she says, leaning into me. "You keep surprising me, you know that?"

"Good. I plan to keep doing that," she smiles, brushing a strand of hair from her face. "So, what's the plan? We finish packing, move to the farm, and then you turn a raccoon nest into my dream teahouse?"

"Exactly," I say. "We'll evict the raccoons gently, of course. Maybe even leave a little welcome gift for their new digs."

She shakes her head, laughing again. "You're unbelievable."

I take her hands. "You're going to love it, Ophelia. I promise."

She holds my gaze, and for a moment, the rest of the world doesn't exist. "I already do."

I kiss her, quick but firm, then let go with a grin. "Alright, enough procrastinating. Go finish packing before I change my mind and bring every single box of random wrenches."

"Only if you promise to throw out those textbooks," she calls over her shoulder as she walks out of the room.

"Deal," I say, shaking my head as I return to the half-packed box on the counter. Her words linger long after she was gone. It isn't just about moving boxes or renovating barns but building something real with her.

Something that feels like home in every sense of the word. *Home.*

Chapter Twenty-Eight

OPHELIA

The house is quiet tonight, quieter than it had ever been. Every sound—the creak of the floorboards, the fridge hum, the occasional rustle of the breeze against the windows—feels amplified, like the house is speaking to me one last time.

It had been my home for as long as I could remember. Tomorrow, though, I will begin to call somewhere else *home*. Emmett and I were moving to the farm, starting the next chapter of our lives together. The bags were packed and stacked neatly by the front door, and the house was bare. It felt less like a home now and more like a memory.

I sat on the worn window seat in the living room, cradling a cup of tea in my hands. Outside, the woods stand dark and steady, like they are guarding over my childhood. The teahouse is closed for now, the little sign Emmett painted for me swinging gently in the breeze: Relocating.

It's strange not having the usual rhythm of my day—no tea to brew, no pastries to bake, no neighbors to greet. There is space to breathe for the first time in years, and it's both freeing and terrifying.

A soft knock on the doorframe pulls me from my thoughts.

Emmett is leaning against the doorway, his hands shoved in his pockets and an easy smile on his face.

"Hey," he says. "You doing okay?"

I nod, though my throat feels tight. "Just . . . processing, I guess."

He steps into the room, his gaze sweeping over the packed boxes and empty shelves. "Yeah, I figured. Big changes, huh?"

"That's an understatement," I say with a shaky laugh. He sits down beside me, his knee brushing mine. For a moment, neither of us says anything, just listening to the house's quiet.

"I get it," he says finally. "This place means a lot to you. You've built your whole life here."

I nod, my fingers tightening around my cup. "It's not just the house, though. It's who I've been here. It's safe, you know? Predictable."

"And now everything's changing," he says gently.

"Exactly," he reaches over and removes the cup from my hand, setting it on the windowsill. Then he intertwines my hands in his, his thumbs brushing over my knuckles. "I know it's scary, Ophelia. But you're not doing this alone. We're in this together, okay?"

My eyes are stinging as I meet his gaze. "What if I'm not ready? What if I mess it up?"

He smiles, that lopsided grin that always makes my heart skip a beat. "So what? We all mess up. Do you remember what you told me? We have each other now." His words touch something inside me, and I let out a shaky breath. "You always know what to say, don't you?"

"Not always," he says. "But I know this—I love you. And no matter where or what we're doing, that will not change."

My breath hitches, and I kiss him before I can overthink it. It starts slow and soft, letting the day's tension melt away, and something deeper take over. Emmett's hands glide up to cradle my face, his thumbs brushing my cheeks as he deepens the kiss. That familiar warmth spread through me, but tonight, it's different—more urgent, more intense.

He drags me onto his lap, and I go willingly, my fingers threading through his hair. His touch firm but gentle. His lips trail down my neck, leaving a trail of heat in their wake.

"Ophelia," he murmurs against my skin, his voice low and full of need.

"Mm?" I manage, but my mind is foggy with sensation.

"I think," he says, his hands trailing down my waist. "That we should properly say goodbye to this house."

I laugh, the sound breathless and shaky. "That's what you're thinking about right now?"

His grin is wick as he pulls back just enough to meet my eyes. "No, but it's a good excuse."

I roll my eyes, but I can't stop smiling. "You're something else, Cowboy."

"And you love it," he says, his lips capturing mine again. The rest of the night passes in a blur of tangled sheets and eagerness. The day's weight melts away as we lose ourselves in each other. When I finally drift off to sleep, curled up against Emmett with his arms around me, the house doesn't feel quite so empty anymore.

Tomorrow would be the start of something new. But tonight, I let myself hold on to what was one last time.

Chapter Twenty-Nine

EMMETT

Ophelia's hands are searching for mine under the covers. I reach out instinctively, threading my fingers through hers as I open one eye to the soft morning light creeping through the curtains.

Today was the day. Move-in day. I stay still for a moment, not wanting to wake her just yet.

Last night had been . . . a lot. Emotional, bittersweet, and beautiful all at once. She said goodbye to this house in her own way, and I'd been there for every second of it—every tear, every memory she shared, and every laugh that bubbled up between the heavier moments. And when words failed, well, we found other ways to connect. Ways that left us breathless and tangled in each other until the early morning hours.

She stirs beside me, tugging the blanket closer to her face before slowly opening her eyes. A sleepy grin stretches across her lips. "Good morning, Cowboy."

"Morning, Sweetheart," I say with a smirk. "After last night, I should be calling you *cowgirl*."

Her cheeks flush a beautiful shade of red, and I swear I melt right there. She has no idea what she does to me. The way her lips quirk, her eyes soften, and that blush creeping across her face—she drives me absolutely insane, and I am addicted.

I playfully tugged at the blanket. She lets out a yelp, grabbing it back in a panic. "Emmett! It's cold!"

I laugh, leaning back against the pillow. "Come on, Sweetheart. Today's the day. Early bird gets the worm, remember?"

She buries her face in the blanket, groaning dramatically. "B-but . . . I don't even like worms, Emmett."

I glance at her, and damn, she's so cute.

Her hair is a messy halo around her face. Her cheeks are still a soft pink from sleep, and a little patch of drool has dried on one side. One sock clung to her foot, while the other had gone missing somewhere in the sheets. She's chaos wrapped in a blanket, and I love every inch of her.

"Well," I say, letting my voice soften. "Lucky for you, I've got breakfast on the way. Should be here soon."

Her face lights up, her smile widening as she sits up slightly. "Breakfast? What kind?"

"Your favorites," I tease, watching her expression grow hopeful. "But we're gonna have company, so you might want to hide those." I gesture toward her bare chest.

"Oh, hush." She yanks the blanket up higher, her voice a mock whisper of indignation. "But this company . . ." Her brows furrow in confusion. "Who is it?"

I watch her, letting the suspense hang in the air before finally answering. "Your mom."

Her face shifts through several emotions in the span of a second—confusion melting into relief and then something deeper, more vulnerable. "You . . . you thought of that?"

"I figured it might be easier," I say, brushing a stray strand of hair behind her ear. "Leaving this house is hard enough. I thought maybe having someone here who understands what you're feeling could help." Her eyes shimmer, and she leans in, kissing my cheek softly. "You're too good to me, Emmett."

"Damn right I am, Mossgrove," I tease, pulling her closer. "But you're worth it."

The sound of the doorbell breaks the moment, and Ophelia groans, flopping back onto the bed.

"Guess that's breakfast," I say, smirking. "Better cover up before your mom sees more of you than she ever wanted to."

She throws a pillow at me, laughing despite herself. "Go get the food, Cowboy. I'll make myself decent."

I grin, grabbing a shirt on my way out of the bedroom. As I head for the door, I can't help but smile. Today was the start of something new—something messy and beautiful and ours. And I wouldn't have it any other way.

The last bite of pancakes lingers in my mouth as I push the empty plate away, my fingers still wrapped around the coffee mug. Ophelia is upstairs, taking a moment, the day's weight pressing on both of us. Her mom, as usual, is the calm in the storm. We've barely spoken a word to each other, just exchanged smiles and the occasional chuckle.

Breakfast is a rare moment of peace before the day fully begins.

"Here," Ophelia's mom says, breaking the silence. She pushes a small velvet box across the table toward me. Her hands steady, her expression unreadable. I stare at the box, confused, unsure what to make of it. The delicate weight of it in my palm feels significant, as if it had been waiting for this moment.

"Open it," she says, her voice soft but firm. I lift the lid carefully, and inside, nestling on a bed of dark velvet, is a simple yet beautiful ring—gold, worn but polished, with a delicate diamond at its center. It isn't large, nothing flashy, but something about it felt . . . timeless. I look up at her, bewildered.

"What is this?" I ask, my voice a little hoarse. Her gaze met mine, steady and direct, as if she is saying something she had known for a long time but was now ready to share.

"My wedding ring," she says, her voice softening as her eyes gloss over. "He wanted it to be hers when the time came."

I swallow hard, my mind reeling. This was his ring to give . . . now passed down for me to give.

Her father, the man who had loved her unconditionally, now entrusted me with a piece of him—a ring that had once been his. It wasn't just a symbol of his love for her, but of the life I was about to step into, with her by my side. She leans in slightly, her tone lowering, a touch of emotion creeping into her voice.

"I want you to have it. It's not just about the ring. It's about what it means. This is where forever starts, Emmett. Do it right." Her words hang in the air, thick with meaning. Not just a blessing—but a call to action. A promise from someone who had seen both the beauty and the heartbreak of love.

My heart pounds in my chest as I process what she said. Her words echo in my mind: Don't wait too long. A realization hits me. This is it. The time is now. I've spent so long figuring out how to make it all work. How to navigate the logistics and the uncertainty, but it was always about us. About Ophelia. And now, I understand. I am not just moving in with her. I am committing to her. To us.

I glance at the ring again, my fingers brushing its smooth surface. Something deep inside me clicks, a feeling I've avoided for months—maybe years. The idea of a future with Ophelia no longer feels like a distant dream. It is tangible, real, and in my hands. Ophelia's mom watches me quietly, a soft smile playing on her lips.

"You'll know when it's time," she says gently. I nod, my

mind racing with the weight of her words. I don't have all the answers, but I know one thing for sure. I am not going to wait.

She stands up and smooths her blouse as she gestures towards the stairs. "I think it's time for me to go upstairs," she says, a slight tremor in her voice. "There's one last thing she needs to do before you two head out."

She didn't need to say anything—her eyes spoke volumes. I can see it in how she holds herself, in the slight trembling of her hand. As they leave for the stairs, I stay behind, sitting in the quiet of the kitchen, staring at the ring in my hand. A few moments passed before I can gather myself enough to follow.

Chapter Thirty

OPHELIA

It feels like the world is holding its breath. For two years, this door remained locked, the key turned in a way that signaled the finality of things—things that could never be changed and would never be the same again.

This finality presses heavily on my chest as I stand beside my mother, watching her fumble with the key in her trembling hands. She had been so strong for so long, but now, in the quiet, the silence between us was full of things unsaid.

My hand hovers at my side, unsure of what to do with itself. I had been waiting for this moment—this inevitable moment when the past would finally be unlocked and let loose. The house is changing, my life is changing, and it feels like it is all happening too fast.

"We don't have to do this right now," I whisper, my voice barely louder than the wind outside. My mother pauses, her fingers curling around the key, her knuckles pale and strained. She doesn't answer me immediately. She stands there, staring at the door in front of us as if it were some kind of portal, a passageway between the past and whatever would come next.

Finally, she looks at me, her eyes soft but determined. "No,

Sweetheart," she said gently, her voice cracking, but there is strength in it, too. "It's time."

It not an easy decision, I know that. It had never been easy for her. In the two years since my father passed, we kept this room locked away, a sacred space where his presence still lingered like a ghost, where the air still carried the scent of his aftershave, and his old boots sat by the door as if he would walk back in any minute.

But he wouldn't. And my mother knew that . . . I knew that.

She slides the key into the lock, her movements slow, careful, as though every turn of the key required some monumental effort. There's a subtle shake in her hands as the lock clicks open, and for a moment, I think I can hear her heartbeat in the silence. With a soft sigh, she pushes the door open, the creak of the hinges loud in the stillness of the house. My heart beats harder in my chest, and I am frozen, unsure if I am ready to step into this room.

This room—my childhood home, my father's domain, where memories clung to the walls like dust—like a living thing, a piece of the past preserved in time, a shrine to what had been lost.

My mother steps in first, and I follow her, my feet heavy with what I am about to see. The air in the room is thick, laden with memories I am not sure I want to relive.

I stand at the door for a moment, feeling the pulse of the house around me, and then I step inside. The room is the same as it had been the day my father died. The bed, where he had taken his last breath, still made the way he had left it— untouched, the sheets perfectly pressed as if he were only sleeping, as if he would wake up any moment and sit up, rubbing his eyes. His pillow still had the imprint of his head, the indent from the weight of his dreams.

I can still smell him in the room—his cologne, a faint trace of woodsmoke, the scent of his work boots. A smell so strong it almost chokes me. I to steady myself against the doorframe as I try to process what I see. My father's clothes still draped over the frame at the foot of the bed, waiting. His boots, his jacket, the hat he wore every day of his life—still there as if he would walk through that door and pick them up again.

The truth hits me like a wave. He's not coming back. I blink, trying to push back the tears threatening to rise, but they can't be kept at bay. Not here. Not in this room that held so many pieces of him.

I swallow hard, my throat closing, and look away from the pile of clothes. "Mom . . ." My voice cracks, and I don't know what to say.

She is at the foot of the bed now, her fingers trailing along the edge of the comforter, her gaze distant, lost. She doesn't answer me right away. Instead, she walks around the bed to her side, where the space had been untouched for so long. Her side of the bed, where she had spent countless nights beside him, was still as he had left it—her pillow exactly where it always was, the small dent in the middle still there as if waiting for her to curl up beside it.

She sits down slowly, her movements careful as though grief might crush her if she moves too quickly. I don't move my hands clasping in front of me, unsure whether to approach her or leave her to her mourning. But then she reaches for his pillow. She holds it close to her chest, pressing it against her face, and I can hear her inhaling deeply as though breathing in the last remnants of him.

"Oh, Willie," she whispers. The words are broken, raw, and heart-wrenching. The sound of her crying—deep, guttural sobs that seem to come from the very core of her—is the most painful thing I have ever heard. The sound of a woman who had lost her best friend, her partner, her everything.

It is the sound of a heart breaking. I want to comfort her. I want to tell her it will be okay, that she didn't have to be strong anymore, but I can't find the words. Instead, I just stand there, a silent witness to her grief. It takes a moment before I can move and finally approach her. Slowly, I kneel beside her, placing a hand on her shoulder, the touch gentle, a wordless offering of support.

Her body trembling under my touch. All those years of unspoken sorrow finally breaking free. We sit like that for what feels like an eternity. No rushing this. No way to hurry through this part of the process. This moment is hers, and I wouldn't take it from her.

Finally, she lets go of the pillow and sets it back on the bed, her eyes brimming with tears. Wiping them away with the back of her hand, her face flush and raw. She takes a deep breath, steadying herself, before turning to me.

"I thought I would never be able to come in here again," she says quietly, her voice hoarse. "I thought it would break me."

I didn't know what to say, so I just nod. "I know, Mom. I know."

But as she stands up, she peers around the room, her gaze soft, almost wistful. "I think he would want us to let go," she says, her voice gaining strength. "I think he would want us to move forward."

Her words hit me harder than I expect. It isn't just about the house, the room, or the clothes left behind. It is about us—about the living, the ones who still had time left to make something of the life that we had. It is about moving forward, even when the past tries to keep pulling us back.

"I think you're right," I whisper, swallowing the lump in my throat. "It's time to say goodbye."

My mother looks at me, her eyes filled with a mixture of sadness and acceptance, and for the first time since my father died, I see something in her eyes that I haven't seen in a long time—peace. She nods, and together, we turn towards the door. We don't look back.

We didn't need to.

As we exit the room, something shifts inside me. The past hadn't gone away, and it never would. But today, we made room for something else. For a future that didn't require holding on to the past, a future where my mother and I could move forward, no longer shackled by the memories that had kept us locked in place.

The door closes behind us with a soft click, and I know, at that moment, that it's time to leave.

The past was behind us now, and I was ready for whatever came next.

Chapter Thirty-One

EMMETT

My truck's engine hums steadily, the rhythmic rumble of the road beneath us grounding me. Beside me, Ophelia sits in her usual spot, close but just far enough to leave room for the invisible distance we haven't quite crossed yet.

She isn't quite herself—her fingers fidgeting in her lap, twisting and tugging at the hem of her sweater, her gaze darting between the road ahead and the scenery around us. Her eyes are wide, her lips pulled into a smile equal parts excitement and nerves, and I can practically feel her energy radiating across the space between us.

I can't help but glance at her more often than I'd like to admit. The way she sits, shoulders hunching forward, eyes sparkling with that mix of anticipation and trepidation—it is beautiful in a way I can't quite put into words.

Something about her presence makes everything else feel secondary. It isn't just her looks—though, damn, she looks like she could light up the whole world. It is how she feels, how she made *me* feel, even on the quietest of drives.

"You okay?" I ask, keeping my voice light and a little teasing. She glances at me, her hands stopping their fidgeting momentarily as her lips curve upward.

"I'm fine," she says, but I can hear the slight tremor in her voice. "Just . . . thinking."

I chuckle softly, my eyes returning to the road, even though I am pulled toward her like a magnet. "Thinking? About what?"

Ophelia hesitates, biting her lower lip. "I don't know," she says with a breathless laugh. "It's just so . . . so much. I've never done anything like this before. You know?" Her words come out in a flurry like she is trying to catch up with the rapid-fire thoughts racing through her mind. "This whole . . . moving thing. The barn, the house, all of it. It feels so big."

I shoot her a sideways glance. "It is big, Ophelia. But big doesn't mean bad." I grin, trying to lighten the moment, knowing she needs something to take her mind off the looming shift in her life. "Besides, you can always hide in the pantry if it gets too big for you. I'll make sure it's stocked with all the teas you can handle."

That makes her laugh, a genuine burst of sound that shook the quiet air between us. She turns to me, her eyes sparkling with something far beyond mere amusement. "I'm going to need way more than tea to get through this," she teases, her voice a little breathless from laughter.

"Trust me," I say with a wink, "I'm sure I can find a few things to help keep you occupied when the tea runs out." Her smile softens into something warmer, her eyes searching mine for a moment. It is subtle—just a fleeting glance—but it is enough.

The truck rolls on, and the familiar landscape around Havenwood slowly gives way to the quieter stretch of road leading us to the farm. The trees are thicker here, their branches stretching high above, their leaves turning shades of orange and gold as autumn begins to stretch its arms across the land. It feels like the place is waiting for us. There's a certain peace in the air, a quiet hum of anticipation that matches the flutter in my chest.

As I drive, I let my mind wander, my thoughts landing on her. I knew this moment was coming, the moment she would leave her childhood home behind and her life would change. But what I hadn't fully understood was how it would change me. She's always been a part of my world, a fixture in the background of my thoughts, even when I was away. I had built my life without considering how much she was woven into its fabric. I thought we had always been on parallel paths, running side by side but never quite crossing.

Even when we'd been at odds, even when I thought I wanted something else, the truth was, it had always been Ophelia. It was always her. She was the one I returned to, the one I couldn't shake, even after all these years.

I grip the steering wheel a little tighter, a wave of realization crashing over me. It was never just about the teahouse, or the festival, or the barn. It was about this.

About us. As we near the end of the gravel road, the farmhouse and barn come into view, sitting quietly at the end of a long stretch of land. The house is old, with weathered wood and a sturdy charm that spoke of years gone by. The barn, though—our barn—is the focal point. It stands like a beacon, ready for the changes we have planned. Changes to give it a new life.

I can't help but grin. "You ready for this?"

I ask, glancing at Ophelia, who is now staring out the window, her breath fogging up the glass.

She nods, her fingers nervously tapping the edge of her seat. "I think so."

I pull the truck onto the gravel driveway, the crunch of the tires underfoot a comforting sound, signaling we have arrived. The space ahead of us feels massive—ours—the open fields stretching beyond the barn, the house a little smaller in comparison but still standing tall, like a guardian of everything that has come before. It is a place full of potential but also full of history.

I threw the truck in park, turning to her with a wide grin. "Well, Sweetheart, this is it. This is where the magic happens. And by 'magic,' I mean manual labor, which, you know, is much less glamorous but just as necessary."

Ophelia rolls her eyes, but the smile she gives me is radiant. "You're impossible."

I can feel the tension coiled inside her slowly begin to relax. She leans back in her seat, letting out a deep breath. "It's beautiful," she says quietly, her gaze wandering over the land. "It's exactly how I imagined it."

Her words hit me deeper than I expect. As if I had been waiting for her to finally see it, to see the vision we'd been working toward.

"I'm glad you like it." I turn off the engine, the stillness of the moment hanging between us. For a moment, it is just us. No more packing, no more worries. Just the sound of the wind rustling through the trees and the soft creak of the barn in the distance.

Then, breaking the silence, I lean towards her with a sly grin. "Hey, I have a question for you," I say, my voice low and teasing.

She turns toward me, raising an eyebrow. "What?"

I shrug nonchalantly, though my grin can't be contained. "Do you know why the scarecrow won an award?"

Her face scrunches up in confusion, and I can tell she is trying to work through the punchline.

I can't resist. "Because he was outstanding in his field."

Ophelia's laughter erupts, a deep belly laugh that makes her whole body shake, her eyes sparkling with delight. Her infectious giggles fill the air, and I feel myself fall for her all over again. Something about that laugh, that unguarded joy, that always gets me.

I sit there, watching her, realizing that this—her—is

exactly what I have been waiting for. It isn't just about building something new together. It's about finally having her where she belonged—with me.

"Okay, that was terrible," she says, wiping tears of laughter from her eyes. "But you know what? I'll let it slide because you've got a barn to renovate."

I grin back, feeling that invisible string between us tighten even further. "Hey, if it makes you laugh, I'll tell terrible jokes for the rest of my life."

I open the truck door, the crisp morning air hitting me like a wave as I step onto the gravel driveway. Ophelia follows close behind, her eyes scanning the scene before us, taking in everything. The house, the barn, the land—it is all so much more real now. So much more ours. I glance at her, smiling, then turn to the flurry of activity around us.

The movers are already hard at work, wheeling boxes into the barn, unloading furniture from trucks, and sorting through everything we'd packed over the past few weeks. It is a bit chaotic, but the energy feels . . . right. James is already getting his hands dirty, lifting a couch with one of the movers.

He sees me and gives a casual wave, his smile as wide as ever. "You're here," he says, chuckling as he straightens up from the couch. "About time."

"Yeah, yeah. Things are moving faster than I expected," I reply, rubbing my hands together in preparation for the work ahead. "You know I can't let you do everything alone, right?"

James gives me an exaggerated look of concern. "Well, someone had to do the heavy lifting. Didn't want you to get too excited."

I laugh, punching him lightly on the shoulder as I move to

help. But before I can make it over, I notice my dad off in the distance, leaf blower in hand, working his way across the patio. His sleeves rolled up, his worn-out boots scuffing the stone, his body moving with the kind of determination only he knew.

I smile. He is in his element here, always getting his hands dirty, always keeping things running. Ophelia notices, too. She looks over at my dad, her eyes softening.

"He looks right at home," she says, her voice filled with affection and admiration.

I nod, appreciating the truth in her words. "Yeah. This place has a way of doing that to people." As if on cue, my sister, Morgan, came into view from the garden with a mischievous smile as she toys with something in the flowerbeds. Her hands are covered in dirt, but there is no sign of her caring as she stands and brushes herself off. She sees us and waves, a teasing look crossing her face.

"Finally, here?" Morgan calls out, raising an eyebrow as she joins them. "I mean, I've been here forever. It's about time you made it to your own move-in day."

Ophelia shoots me a knowing look, and I roll my eyes. "Don't mind her. She's just happy that she gets to boss me around now."

Morgan chuckles, shaking her head. "You make it sound like you never let me." She turns her attention to Ophelia. "I am so excited to have you as part of the family now."

Ophelia smiles, her eyes sparkling. "I am excited to be family now." Her words hit me harder than I expect. Hearing her say it out loud, hearing her feel it—like she wasn't just here as a guest or visitor, but as someone who belonged— made my chest tighten in the best way possible.

This was our home.

I watch Ophelia and Morgan chat, the sound of my dad in the background, James still hauling boxes. The whole scene is chaotic, yes, but it is also peaceful in its own way. The kind of noise that feels familiar, comforting, like it's all supposed to be happening.

Ophelia catches my gaze again, a smile softening her features as she steps closer. "I think I'm going to like it here," she says, her voice barely above a whisper.

I grin, wrapping an arm around her. "Me too."

As we made our way towards the barn, the world around us feels like it's falling into place. The barn is no longer just a building on a piece of land—it is a future—her future. Our future. James gives me a quick nod as we pass him, his eyes sharp as always, but his smile never falters. My dad waves from the patio, his attention still fixed on the task at hand, but there is a glimmer of approval in his expression.

It feels right.

We reach the barn, the old wooden structure standing tall against the sky, its weathered exterior seeming to welcome us in. The door is slightly ajar, and movers are carrying boxes inside. Ophelia stops at the threshold, taking it all in.

This will be her new teahouse, the start of something healthy. I take her hand, squeezing it gently. "Ready for the next part?" I ask, my voice low but full of meaning.

Ophelia smiles, her eyes searching mine for a long moment. "Ready," she says, her voice steady, but her heart still unsure and nervous.

I don't let go of her hand. "Good. Because we're doing this together. Every step, Little Lady."

She nods, and I see the full weight of her trust in me. I have no idea where the road ahead will take us, but I know one thing with complete certainty—I want it. I want it all.

As we navigate to the farmhouse, the sounds of life and laughter surrounding us, I realize that no matter how much change has come, this is exactly where we were meant to be— right here, right now.

Chapter Thirty-Two

OPHELIA

T he night settles around us, the house still humming with the remnants of the day's commotion. The movers were gone, the last of the boxes and furniture tucked neatly into corners. Emmett had gone outside to check on something, leaving me alone to unpack and make this place feel like home. Though filled with all the newness of our beginnings, the house seems to have been waiting for me.

I am not in a rush, not really. There is a calmness in the air now, a stillness that allows me to breathe without feeling rushed or overwhelmed. I move through the kitchen, sorting through dishes, organizing the cabinets, and stacking cups with a quiet sense of satisfaction. My fingers graze over the edges of each cup. The delicate porcelain is still unfamiliar to me, but it is already a part of the new routine I am starting to create.

I love the way everything fits. Everything finds its place. My life here is slowly taking shape, becoming something I can hold in my hands. My record player, plugged in courtesy of my mom's thoughtful gesture, spins its soft tunes on the island. The sound of the crackling vinyl fills the space, warm and nostalgic, wrapping around me like an old, familiar hug.

It creates a rhythm for me, a heartbeat for the house that makes everything feel right. Poe and Gunner are playing together at my feet. Gunner had found a squeaky toy. He is determined to chew it into oblivion while Poe nuzzles him occasionally, trying to get him to chase.

Their little antics make me smile and feel light, like everything is falling into place. The way they dart around my legs and tumble over each other brings a sense of life to the stillness of the room. It wasn't just the house changing—it was me, too. I can feel it in my bones, this sense of something new stirring within me.

I turn to the cabinet, reaching up to place the teacups I had carefully packed. They fit perfectly beside Emmett's beer glasses. I don't have to think twice about it. They belonged here, in this house, even if it is all still new. The ritual of putting them in their place is like a promise—one I made to myself, to him, to the life we are building together.

I let the sound of the music guide me, making me feel like I am dancing through the motions of something sacred, something timeless. The soft, crackling vinyl echoes through the kitchen, and as the song picks up, so do I. I let myself get caught in its rhythm, feeling the beat pulse through me like a heartbeat, a quiet vibration that makes everything feel free.

My hips sway as I hum, and a soft giggle escapes my lips. Something about this house and this new chapter makes me stretch my arms wide, unfurl myself, and just be. It isn't about making the home perfect or settling everything. It's about me, here, finally allowing myself to feel the freedom that has eluded me for so long.

I close the cabinet door and turn back to the island, my hands still moving to the rhythm of the music. I spin, letting my arms stretch wide, surrendering to the music, to the moment. My feet shuffle across the floor, unsure but excited, the faintest smile curling at the corners of my lips. I move slowly at first, just a gentle sway as I let myself get lost in the melodies, feeling the warmth of the music creep up my spine. But as the song picks up, so do my steps. I twirl around the kitchen, my movements growing more fluid with each turn.

A quiet laugh escapes me, a slight sound of happiness bubbling up from deep inside. It is a laugh I don't recognize at first—laughter that is light and full of joy, not burdened by years of uncertainty or fear. My heart is full of something I haven't felt in a long time. It makes me want to dance, laugh, and live.

I am free. I am truly, finally, free. The kitchen is no longer just a space for cooking meals or making tea. It has become mine, a place where I can shed the dust of my past and embrace everything ahead. The sound of the music—like a thread, pulls me into a future that is waiting for me, waiting for both of us. I twirl, arms wide, and laugh again—loud, uncontained.

And this time, I let myself feel every moment of it. I was dancing into a new life I'd never thought I could have. I am here, doing it. The music spins on, the records turning, and with each note, each moment, I can feel the house filling with more than just furniture. It's filled with me, my heart and soul, and everything I have left to give.

The music wraps around me, embracing me in a way that words never could, as if it knows that this is the beginning of something bigger, something more. I am not just unpacking boxes. I am unpacking myself.

I can hear Poe and Gunner's playful growls as they chase each other around, the sound of their paws clicking against the wood floor making me smile.

They are here with me, just like Emmett. With the music, love, and joy in this house, I can feel a piece of my soul settle into its rightful place.

The music moves me again. As I spin, I turn to see Emmett on one knee, tears streaming down his sweet, sweet face. *Emmett.*

"Marry me, little lady, marry me and love me forever." The words fall out of his mouth, hitting me like a soft breeze. I freeze mid-spin, eyes wide. My heart stopped for a moment before it picks up again, racing in my chest. The world seems to slow around me, and for a brief moment, everything disappears except for him—there, on one knee, with that same mischievous yet tender smile tugging at his lips.

The room, the music, and the laughter from earlier fade into the background as I focus on the one thing that matters: him. I face him fully, still processing the words that hang between us like a promise. Emmett looks up at me, his eyes soft but intense, filled with something I can only describe as complete certainty.

The playful teasing always in his gaze had melted away, replaced with something deeper, more profound—something I can't quite put into words but know I recognize in every inch of his being. And then I see it—the ring. It is a small box, the velvet surface catching the light in a way that made my breath catch. He holds it out toward me, his hand steady, his posture resolute. It sparkles faintly under the kitchen lights, its presence both grounding and overwhelming.

Mom's ring.

I am breathless, my hands trembling. My whole body seems frozen in time, suspended in this beautiful, surreal moment, like something out of a dream. The reality of what is happening washes over me in waves. Emmett is here, on one knee, asking me to marry him.

I take a tentative step forward, almost as if I fear this moment might slip through my fingers if I move too quickly. Each step is impossibly slow and achingly fast, the anticipation building in my chest as I close the distance between us. The closer I get, the more my pulse races, and my heart soars.

Every little part of me wants to reach out and pull him to me, but I am rooted to the spot, captivated by the moment's beauty. Emmett's eyes never leave mine. I can see the warmth there, the love building between us, quietly, steadily, until it had reached this point. I wasn't sure when it happened—when the shift occurred when the invisible string that had always connected us together had tied its knot.

But standing here at this moment, it is so clear. It's always been him. And in the same breath, it's always been me. Two halves of something whole, spending forever together as if it's the most natural thing in the world.

I stop before him, my breath coming faster now, my voice shaky as I finally speak.

"Emmett . . ." I whisper, my voice barely audible over the music playing in the background. I swallow, trying to collect myself, but the emotions are too raw, too overwhelming. "I don't even know what to say."

He chuckles softly, his smile widening. "I'm just waiting for you to say yes, Little Lady."

I nod, my throat tight. *Yes.* The word seems so simple, yet so monumental right now. How can I even begin to express everything I feel in a single word? But in my heart, I already know the answer. It has always been yes.

"I . . . yes," I manage to say, my voice barely above a whisper. "Yes, Emmett," I scream.

And just like that, the world shifts again. The words were out, and everything else fell into place. Emmett's face lit up, and before I know it, his arms are around me, lifting me off the ground as he pulls me into a soft and gentle kiss. It's full of everything we have been building. I can feel the warmth of his love, the certainty of his touch, as though this moment, this decision, was the one we had been waiting for all along.

When he pulls away, his face is beaming, and I can't stop the tears in my eyes.

"I love you," he says, his voice low and sincere. "I'm so damn lucky."

I smile, brushing away a stray tear, my hands finding his. "I love you, too," I whisper back, feeling a peace settle over me like I am finally exactly where I am meant to be. The thought makes my heart swell as I slide the ring onto my finger.

It is real. It is happening.

This is it. This is the rest of our lives, beginning right here, in this kitchen and house that will slowly become our home.

"What if everything changes?" I whisper, half to myself, as I look at him.

Emmett catches the murmur, glancing down at me with a curious smile. But instead of waiting for him to answer, I take a deep breath, tilting my head to the ceiling. As he holds me, I know the answer . . .

I welcome the change.

Acknowledgments

No journey is taken alone, no dream woven without threads of love and support. This book exists because of my cherished village, the fellow writers who have helped me rise above my fear and limits, and my readers who have taught me the meaning of authenticity and having confidence in myself. Thank you, your love is my constant compass.

Brittany Tucker, you have been my unwavering saving grace. From your breathtaking writing to your inspiring words of belief and guidance, your impact runs deeper than words can express. No one will ever truly understand the seeds you've sown—nurturing my heart, my career, and my life in ways that continue to blossom.

Breanna, thank you for always being my greatest cheerleader. From our late-night phone calls and early-morning chats to everything in between, your support has been a constant source of strength. You've shown me the true meaning of dedication, and your unwavering encouragement carried me through every late night and every blank page.

Halie Riley, thank you for bringing so many of my dreams to life through this book. Your dedication to creating the map and art prints for my story is a gift I will forever treasure.

Mom and Dad, thank you for being the ultimate example of a strong, healthy relationship—a love that stands firm through every storm. Most of all, thank you for always welcoming me home to heal in the warmth and safety of that love.

Bitty, you have always been the embodiment of pure talent—a delicate leaf swaying gracefully in the wind, the soothing melody of angels singing a lullaby. Your beautiful presence fills any room with peace and ease. Thank you for reminding me to slow down, embrace nature, stay true to myself, and always find time to laugh. I miss you deeply. (You too, Jeff, thank you for being such a great beacon of love, laughter, and adventure in my life.)

Caity, my first best friend, my JWoww, my tater bater—you are everything I aspire to be. Graceful, successful, overflowing with love and determination, and the perfect balance of strength and independence. Thank you for making my childhood a haven and for always having my back, both physically and verbally. You are a gift.

Gage, my sweet husband, thank you for mending the parts of me you didn't break. You've been a guiding light through every dark tunnel, standing strong beside me when I tremble and lifting me to feel the sun again. It was always you, cowboy.

Lastly, and most importantly, Theodore, Olivia, and Mason—my sun, my moon, and my stars. Thank you for being the anchors that keep me grounded, for making me a mommy and an auntie, and for inspiring the child in me to sing. I love you three with every fiber of my being. May you one day find a love that makes you smile like a fool and dance in the kitchen at 3 AM.

Oh, wait . . . you didn't think I forgot about you, did you, David? Thank YOU for being the closest thing to stability in my life. You've loved me through my most challenging moments, supported me during my wildest times, and given me a home when I was at my lowest. You have always been my family, and for that, Emmett is a reflection of you—Davidius, the one who loves the biggest and the best.

Ophelia's Pumpkin Chocolate Chip Cookies

(INSTRUCTIONS WRITTEN BY EMMETT STERLING)

Ingredients you will need:

1 cup canned pumpkin purée (not the pie filling)
1/2 cup unsalted butter, softened
1/2 cup granulated sugar
1/2 cup packed brown sugar
1 large egg
1 teaspoon vanilla extract
2 cups all-purpose flour
1 teaspoon baking soda
1/2 teaspoon salt
1 teaspoon ground cinnamon
1/2 teaspoon ground ginger
1/4 teaspoon ground cloves
1 1/2 cups chocolate chips

Instructions:

Alright, listen up, we've got cookies to make, and let me tell you, these are gonna be legendary. I'm gonna walk you through it, step-by-step, but don't get too distracted. We're here for a good time, and maybe a little bit of chaos—just the right kind, though. **_Let's go!_**

1.Preheat the oven to 350°F (175°C). You'll want it nice and toasty when we get those cookies in. Line a baking sheet with parchment paper—trust me, this is like a cozy little mattress for your cookies to bake on.

2.Grab a large bowl and get your butter all soft and squishy. Now, mix the butter with the granulated sugar and brown sugar until it's all nice and creamy. You want it smooth like velvet, but not too smooth—gotta keep that texture!

3.Next, crack in the egg, splash in the vanilla extract, and then the magical pumpkin purée. Stir it all up until it's well combined, just like you're making a secret potion. Seriously, this is where the magic happens. (_I would know_)

4.Now, in a different bowl (_we don't want chaos just yet_), mix together the flour, baking soda, salt, cinnamon, ginger, and cloves. Get those spices in there—don't skimp, this is what gives the cookies that _wow_ factor.

5.Slowly start mixing the dry ingredients into the wet ingredients. Don't rush it, alright? Stir it just until the dough comes together—no need for extra enthusiasm here. We're making cookies, not a workout routine.

6.Alright, it's chocolate time. Fold in the chocolate chips like you're gently tucking in a blanket on a cold night. But don't overmix! You don't want to ruin the magic, just make sure the chips are scattered throughout, like little treasures in the dough.

7.Scoop tablespoon-sized portions of dough onto your lined baking sheet, leaving a bit of space between them—remember, cookies need their personal space. They'll thank you for it later when they bake up beautifully.

8.Bake for about 10-12 minutes. You'll know they're done when the edges are slightly golden. The centers will be a little soft, but that's exactly what we want for that chewy, melt-in-your-mouth texture. Trust the process!

9.Let the cookies cool on the baking sheet for about 5 minutes. This is key, people! After that, transfer them to a wire rack to cool completely. No rushing here, patience is a virtue.

And there you go! Now, you've got the most delightful, pumpkin-spiced, chocolatey cookies you've ever tasted. Eat 'em warm, eat 'em cold, just enjoy the ride. You nailed it!

Havenwood's Vanilla Bean Scones

(INSTRUCTIONS WRITTEN BY FLORENCE)

Ingredients you will need:

Vanilla Scones:

2 cups all-purpose flour

$\frac{1}{4}$ cup granulated sugar

2 teaspoons baking powder

$\frac{1}{4}$ teaspoon baking soda

$\frac{1}{2}$ teaspoons salt

6 tablespoons cold unsalted butter, cubed

$\frac{1}{2}$ cup cold half and half

1 teaspoon vanilla bean paste (or $\frac{1}{2}$ vanilla bean, or 1 teaspoon vanilla extract)

1 large egg

Additional half and half, for brushing

Coarse sugar, for sprinkling (optional)

Vanilla Icing:

1 cup powdered sugar

1-3 tablespoons half and half

$\frac{1}{2}$ teaspoon vanilla bean paste (or $\frac{1}{2}$ vanilla bean, or $\frac{1}{2}$ teaspoon vanilla extract)

Instructions:

Ah, my dear, it's time to bake something truly splendid! Follow me, and we'll make these scones *so* delicious that even the stars will want a taste. Ready? **Let's begin.**

1.Preheat the oven to 400°F, darling. No rushing this part – we want the oven to be as warm as a summer's day. Line a half or quarter sheet pan with parchment paper. Trust me, it'll make the cleanup a breeze.

2.In a large bowl, combine the flour, sugar, baking powder, baking soda, and a pinch of salt. A little sprinkle of salt never hurt anyone! Then, take your chilled cubed butter and, using a pastry blender (or, if you're feeling dramatic, your trusty hands), cut the butter into the dry ingredients until it's as small as little peas. Yes, I'm serious—tiny little pea-like bits.

3.Now, whisk together the half and half, egg, and that gorgeous vanilla bean paste—oh, the aroma! Add this to the flour mixture and gently mix until the dough begins to come together like a beautiful puzzle. If it gets a little sticky, don't fret; it's just getting cozy.

4.Time to get hands-on! Turn the dough out onto the counter and use your hands to finish forming a uniform dough. No need to be shy now, get in there!

5.Pat the dough to about 1-2 inches thick. Here comes the fun part! Fold one half of the dough over onto the other, like you're tucking it in for a nap. Flatten it again to 1-2 inches thick and repeat the fold and flatten routine 2 more times. I know, it's like a little doughy dance. So satisfying.

6.Now, form the dough into a rough 6-inch square, about 1 inch tall. Don't worry about perfection – think of it as an abstract masterpiece. Cut it into 4 smaller squares, then slice each small square into 2 beautiful triangles.

7.Place the triangles on the prepared sheet pan and brush with more half and half. If you're feeling fancy, sprinkle a bit of coarse salt on top. It's like the perfect little finishing touch.

8.Bake until the scones are a glorious shade of golden brown, both on top and bottom – about 17-20 minutes. Let them cool just a tad while you prepare the icing to crown your creations.

And there you have it, darling! These scones will be the talk of the town. Enjoy!

About the Author

Hailey Renee is an author based in cozy Indiana. Most days, you will find her with a heated blanket, hot tea, and a good book, with her husband and son not far behind. Hailey is a folk practitioner, herbalist, and collector of crystals and vintage treasures.